SICK AND TWISTED

DANNY SALAZAR

iUniverse®

SICK AND TWISTED

This is a work of fiction. All of the characters, names, incidents, organizations, and dialogue in this novel are either the products of the author's imagination or are used fictitiously.

iUniverse books may be ordered through booksellers or by contacting:

iUniverse
1663 Liberty Drive
Bloomington, IN 47403
www.iuniverse.com
1-800-Authors (1-800-288-4677)

Because of the dynamic nature of the Internet, any web addresses or links contained in this book may have changed since publication and may no longer be valid. The views expressed in this work are solely those of the author and do not necessarily reflect the views of the publisher, and the publisher hereby disclaims any responsibility for them.

Any people depicted in stock imagery provided by Getty Images are models, and such images are being used for illustrative purposes only. Certain stock imagery © Getty Images.

ISBN: 978-1-5320-7901-6 (sc)
ISBN: 978-1-5320-8380-8 (hc)
ISBN: 978-1-5320-7905-4 (e)

Library of Congress Control Number: 2019910482

Print information available on the last page.

iUniverse rev. date: 07/24/2019

Contents

Introduction

This second novel, which you are about to read, is more fucked up than the first. I hope all my readers enjoy this book and share it with others. This is a fictional story and is not real in any way. Keep in mind, this novel is for mature readers only, so please do not show it to any easily offended, whiny little bitches.

Thank you and enjoy!

Dirty Old Man

New York City, 2008.

An elderly man and a reckless mob leader who went by the name Edgar sat outside a run-down hotel with the old man's annoying teenage grandson, George, who did nothing but chauffeur him around in his old classic car and bitch and complain about everything.

"What the hell are you doing at this shithole hotel, Grandpa? You have money. Why don't you get yourself a nice room at a Holiday Inn or something?"

Edgar never had any time for wise-ass questions, so he just always told his grandson the real deal.

"Wake up, grandson! This is New York City, you little motherfucker, and the Senton Hotel is the best goddamn hotel in the state! As a matter of fact, it even has some history. This is the same hotel where me and your Grandma made your daddy and the same place where your mama and daddy made you. So please show some respect, okay! Because tonight, your grandpa is going to celebrate his sixty-ninth birthday, and you only turn sixty-nine once, and so that's why I'm here! There is going to be a sexy piece of ass arriving for your grandpa tonight, and I don't need you around to bother me!"

"Does Grandma know about this, Grandpa?" wondered George.

"Hell, no! The bitch doesn't know, and don't go off telling her ether, or I'll kick your fucking teeth in! Besides, she wouldn't care anyway. She's probably at home needing a sweater or something, just like old lady bitches always do!"

"Gee, Grandpa, I can't wait to be like you one day!"

"Don't you worry, grandson. You will one day. You will one day."

After telling his grandson his plans for the night, he quickly sent him on his way home.

"Now go on, kid! My bitch will be arriving any minute, and I don't want her to see me with any kids around!"

"But how are you going to get home, Grandpa?"

"Just pick me up in a couple of hours. I should be done fucking her by then."

After being told that, George hopped in his grandpa's classic Hotchkiss limousine and slowly drove away. The car was very loud and very slow, and George did not like it because it made him stick out like a sore thumb. After leaving his grandpa at the rundown hotel, Edgar quickly walked to the front entrance of the hotel to greet a good friend of his. That friend was a man named Mr. Finger Banger, a crack cocaine dealer and the owner of the Senton Hotel. Old Man Edgar always felt comfortable doing business with him because they were about the same age and had known each other for a long time, and he didn't trust anybody else.

"Well, look who it is! It's Old Man Edgar. Happy birthday, you crazy son of a bitch!" yelled Mr. Finger Banger.

"Oh, thank you so much! I'm now sixty-nine years old, and I'm going to go all out and have myself a good fucking time tonight! I have a sexy lady friend on the way right now, and she is going to bang my brains out all night long. Woohoo! I sure hope my heart doesn't give in again, because last time was a close one. I feel one day I just might die in some pussy from a heart attack, and I wouldn't even feel bad about it at all. Haha."

"I got a new stack of your favorite pleasurable magazines, if you're interested?"

Right away, Edgar knew what he was talking about it. It was their little secret, a calling card to deal crack, like usual. Mr. Finger Banger may have been the Owner of the Senton Hotel, but he also slung crack on the side. He would always treat his costumers with a little something extra, and that extra was, of course, a homemade family porn magazine, photographed and handmade by Mr. Finger Banger himself. He would take pictures of his wife and daughter having sexual intercourse and share it with all his friends in town. Not only that, but he would staple a small bag of crack to the magazine for more excitement and better sales. He even had his own commercial at one time.

"Hey, all you folks out there, this is Mr. Finger Banger presenting you a brand-new stay-at-home magazine called *The Crackle and Jack-o*. Not only do you get a jerk-off magazine, but you get a bag of crack as well! That's right, folks. First we crackle you, and then we jack-o you. So please come down to the Senton Hotel and get your *Crackle and Jack-o* magazine now!"

How is Mr. Finger Banger still in business? I do not know. I guess he is just good at making everybody feel right at home.

"Did you just say, Mr. Finger Banger, that you had a brand-new stack of those wonderful magazines?"

"I sure did, Edgar. Here are five free copies for you, my friend. Happy birthday!"

"Oh, boy. Thank you so much, Mr. Finger Banger. My sexy little lady is going to love this!"

"Did you say you found yourself a sexy lady, Edgar?" asked Mr. Finger Banger.

"Sure did! Found this bitch off the Live Links Hotline, and let me tell you something, man, the Live Links bitches are all desperate and horny as fuck. The one I'm meeting tonight told me she's a single mom, out of work, and always willing to give up a little ass for some change under the table so she can feed those kids."

"Hey, man, ain't nothing wrong with that. A woman got to do what a woman got to do, right?"

"You damn right, Mr. Finger Banger, and God bless all those bitches!"

"What's her name?" asked Mr. Finger Banger.

"Her hood rat name is Coco, because everybody says she will drive you bananas all day and night, but she told me to call her Scarlet instead, just because she says I'm her special little guy."

"Well, she sounds like a real winner, Edgar. Here is the key to your room. I'll direct her over when she arrives."

"Thank you so much, Mr. Finger Banger. You are the best damn friend a guy could ever have."

"Friends till the death, Edgar, friends till the death."

The two men gave each other a friendly hug with a smile on each face, and without speaking a word, they went their separate ways.

When Edgar got to his hotel room, he had to make an important phone call before his beloved Scarlet arrived to fulfill his sexual needs. And that phone call was to his right-hand man, Bugsy, the old lady stalker. He got that name because he enjoyed following old ladies home late at night just to rob them of every penny, and all medications they had on them. Bugsy was always a serious man looking for better opportunities for himself and the rest of the mob, and because of that, he knew that phone call from Edgar was just as important to him as well.

"Hey, Bugsy! Edgar's here. How's everything looking for tomorrow?"

Tomorrow was a big day for Edgar, Bugsy, and the rest of the mob. They were about to invest in a brand-new casino and were only signatures away from ownership.

"I'm doing very good, boss. Can't wait till tomorrow. Everything will change, and once we take full ownership of our own casino, New York City will be ours."

"Hell, yeah! It will be, and so will every whore in town."

"Calm down, boss. I know it's your birthday, and you're at that same old hotel waiting on another skank to have drunken sex with her, but I need you tomorrow morning to pull this deal off, so please don't get to fucked up tonight."

"Don't you worry about me, you son of a bitch! I'll be fine."

"I trust you, boss. I trust you."

They hung up, and Edgar continued to wait for his well-paid piece of ass, Scarlet.

Scarlet's Arrival

Time was winding down, and Edgar was quickly growing impatient as every second went by. "Goddamn! Where is this bitch? I'm only working with two hours here!" shouted Edgar.

Scarlet was just minutes away from the hotel and had lost track of time after making a quick pit stop at the Sticky Fingers Joint, a small restaurant not too far from the Senton Hotel.

"Can't fuck on an empty stomach. I sure hope these s'mores fries and Buffalo balsamic blue chicken poppers don't make me shit during sex!" said Scarlet quietly to herself as she slowly entered the Senton Hotel. Right away, she notified the front desk. "What up, old timer? I'm a guest for a Mr. Edgar."

"Oh yes, my dear. You must be the one and only Scarlet."

"Yes, I am Einstein. Now, where's the room? I don't got all fucking day!"

"Damn, bitch! I love your fast-ass ways. Maybe when you're done with that old bastard, we can get together too?"

"I don't got time for this shit, old timer! Now, where can I find Edgar, you little piece of shit?"

Mr. Finger Banger felt a bit scared but also sexually aroused by Scarlet's loud voice.

"Sorry, miss. I mean no harm. I was just trying to see if I could squeeze in an appointment with you—that's all."

"Well then, today is your lucky day, sir, because I'm giving all new clients free blowjob samples."

"Oh, shit! I guess today is my lucky day!" yelled Mr. Finger Banger with a joyful look on his face.

"If you want your luck to continue to run smoothly, sir, then you might want to tell me what room number I could find Edgar in, because the faster I can be done with him, the quicker I can get with you."

"Room 21, the last door on the right!" said Mr. Finger Banger quickly, reenergized with joy.

"Thank you so much, sir. Now, you hang tight, and when I get back, I'm going to make all your dreams come true. Do you understand me, you little bitch?"

"Oh, miss! I will always be your bitch. You can turn me out anytime you want."

"That's what I like to hear, my new best friend. Now, don't say another word, and I'll be right back in a flash."

Mr. Finger Banger did exactly what Scarlet told him to do. He kept quiet and never spoke a word as he slowly watched her walk away in her tight leather pants and her bright pink high heels. The minute she got to the door, she knocked with a joyful tune, hoping to improve Edgar's mood so she could hear her true apologies for being late. But Edgar wouldn't budge. He was the type of guy who always expected his money's worth.

"What, bitch? You expect me to answer the door with a smile or something? Your ass needs to be on time. I'm not getting any younger!"

"Please, Edgar, relax. Let me make it up to you. I promise, my darlin' you won't leave here the same person you are now. You will be a whole new man."

"You talk a good game, bitch, but you better be right, or I'll just go find myself another whore to replace your little chicken ass!"

Deep down inside, Scarlet began to feel sort of sorry for Old Man Edgar. She didn't want to kill anybody on their birthday, but she felt that she still needed to set an example to make everything right, not just for herself but for the voices screaming in her head as well. Scarlet, a.k.a., Coco, was not the ordinary fast-tailed woman Edgar normally required. This time, Edgar might have bitten off more than he could chew.

"Thank you so much for being late, bitch! I was ready to get down in some pussy a half hour ago, but now my stomach is turned upside down, and so that means now I have to take a huge shit. When I get out, I want to see you laying out but-ass naked on that goddamn bed! Now, do you got that, girl?"

"I hear you loud and clear, baby," Scarlet whispered. And soon as Edgar slammed the bathroom door Scarlet dove into her purse to grab her bloodstained fishing line and a rusted blade that belonged to a bottom of an ice skate, which she always carried on her for her own protection.

"This should show that old fucking billy goat," said Scarlet. Without warning, she kicked off her favorite slut-girl high heels and began kicking the bathroom door with full force, over and over again, until she heard Old Man Edgar screaming with rage.

"Hey! You fucking stupid bitch, you better knock it off, or I'll come out there and beat your motherfucking hooker ass!" yelled Edgar from the inside of his stink-bomb hotel bathroom. But Scarlet wouldn't stop. She kept kicking the door and watching the paint chips fall off little by little. By the looks of the door, you could tell it wasn't too expensive, but it could no longer hold anymore, and as Scarlet continued kicking the old beat-up door, it finally caved in.

"What the fuck you think you're doing, bitch?" yelled Edgar, but it was too late. Scarlet was through the door, and she came right after Edgar while he was sitting there in fear on the leaky toilet bowl.

"Your time is up, old man. Now, give me your fucking money and all the goddamn drugs you got!" shouted Scarlet as she quickly engaged her ice skate blade right through the side of Edgar's left hearing aid, leaving him deaf in one ear.

"Ah, you fucking bitch! What the fuck did you just do?" Edgar cried.

"Keep your fucking mouth shut bitch before I make your mother my whore!" yelled Scarlet.

"She not even alive anymore!" Edgar replied.

"Don't get fucking smart me with me, old man, or I'll take you out back and rape the shit out of your ass!"

And all Edgar could do now was lie in a puddle of his blood as Scarlet began to slowly move up from behind to viciously strangle Edgar to his death with her bloodstained fishing line.

"Just another victim!"

She screamed as she began to dig through the rest of Edgar's pockets, searching for more valuables. But Edgar didn't have much, and so she began kicking Edgar's corpse over and over again until she felt it was no longer necessary. And without any thought upon leaving the body, she grabbed her things and stormed out the hotel room, bitchy and unsatisfied.

THREE
Home Sweet Home

As she walked out of the hotel room, she quickly shut the door behind her so that the smell of the body wouldn't hit the hallways too soon. Looking to her lift, she could see Mr. Finger Banger at his front desk, doing office work all the way down the hall. She was not in the mood to interact with anybody at the moment.

"Fuck, man! I'm not trying to talk to this guy right now!" said Scarlet softly to herself. Now she needed to find another way out the hotel other than walking out the front, so she could avoid the loud and annoying Mr. Finger Banger. And as she began to look around, she immediately noticed the fire escape door. She knew that would set off an alarm, which would draw too much attention, but she didn't care. It had to be done, and she needed to get out of there before anybody found out what she had done inside room 21. Walking out the back door and relieved that she finally got to breathe in fresh air and no longer the stench of cum, piss, and Old Man Edgar's blood, she felt marvelous deep inside. A smile came to her face as she began to sprint as fast as she could on barefoot, with her heels and purse in hand. Not too many people would stop and stare, because it was not always good to be a witness to criminal activity in New York City. You just might have raunchy and violent strangers come looking for you.

After a good fifteen minutes of hard, sweet running, she began to run short of breath and came to a complete stop, looking around in every direction to make sure she was not being followed or watched by anyone or anything. After Scarlet acknowledging her surroundings were safe, she slipped back on her high heels to continue walking all the way to her nearby home, just up the street on Murray Hill.

"Almost fucking home, goddamn it. I need a bath, a joint, and a long, comfortable night of wet pussy masturbation," she said to herself out loud with a firm face and an idiotic clown chuckle.

Her front door wasn't secured very well. The doorknob was missing, and the only thing keeping it shut tight was a dirty Santa Claus stocking cap that had been shoved through the crack of the door. Scarlet wasn't much of a housekeeper, and so dirty bras and panties were lying around the floors and hanging on lamps, shelves, and ceiling fans, while the rest of the place smelled like dead animal, burned pizza, and cigarettes. Scarlet loved living the simple life in her own unusual way, and because of that, she never had any friends. In fact, the only friend she had was her dead cat, Whiskers, who had been hit by a snow plow truck two years ago, which she had been storing under her bed since then. After Whiskers' death, Scarlet claimed his soul had gotten possessed by Heinrich Himmler, the Reichsführer-SS and leading member of Hitler's German Nazi Party. Scarlet also believed she heard voices from her dead cat, calling for her in the middle of the night while she slept alone in her hard, squeaky bed.

"Scar … lett. Hey, bitch! There some real pussy under this bed," shouted Whiskers. But Scarlet wasn't frightened. This was an everyday conversation between a crazy, psychotic bitch and her dead talking cat.

"Shut the fuck up, Whiskers. I'm not trying to hear your shit today!" Scarlet replied angrily.

"How many kills did you get tonight, bitch! How many souls have you captured for me?"

Scarlet strongly believed that the more people she killed for Whiskers, the more souls she could capture for her rising evil spirt, Heinrich Himmler, who would one day relive on this earth.

"I only got to kill one person today, Whiskers! And that's the best I could do, because I didn't have much time!"

"You dumb fucking bitch! How dare you tell me you didn't have enough time!"

"I'm telling you right now, Whiskers, I'm like three seconds from knocking you right through the fucking wall! And you're not going to like it, bitch, when I'm standing over you claiming victory!"

From that very moment, Whiskers knew he had to slow his roll.

"Hey, Scarlet, relax, okay? I'm just trying to prepare my soul to be reborn so I can kill many more deadbeat Jews once again, that's all. Scarlet, I don't mean no other harm."

As Scarlet gazed into Whiskers' bright, sparkling maggot eyes, she grew a softer side of feelings for him, and without giving it any thought, she ran over to his rotted corpse and cradled him in her arms, lying his head against her chest, and began swing him back and forth, singing her favorite lullaby tunes to put him into a deep cat sleep.

"You go back, Jack, do it again. Wheels turning round and round. You go back, Jack, do it again. You like that song, Whiskers? I thought I'd try something different. You're probably sick and tired of hearing that 'Me So Horny' song, huh?"

But Whiskers was already asleep before she knew it, and so to spend the rest of Scarlet's silent and unhappy night, she flipped on her twelve-inch TV to enjoy another episode of her favorite Western television show, *Gunsmoke*.

"Can't watch *Gunsmoke* without a bottle of whiskey!" she yelled as she reached under her bed pillow for the fifth of Kessler. Watching Westerns always made her hungry, but then again, so did the whiskey, and so, by the end of the night, she had already stuffed her face with pinto beans and pork rinds, which made Scarlet fall suddenly asleep next to her beloved dead cat, Whiskers.

Cannibal Mafia

The morning sun rose high and bright throughout the city of New York, and you could smell the fresh breakfast cooking in the air from all the local restaurants. It was seven o'clock, and Bugsy decided to hold an early Irish coffee and doughnut appetizer just before meeting up with their boss, Mr. Edgar. So, at his beloved home, deep in the Bronx, on 183rd Street, four men were gathered around a pigeon-pooped picnic table that was nailed down in the middle of Bugsy's living room, where they would make conversation upon the casino and other ways to invest money. Sometimes their company was hard for Bugsy to put up with, but in the end, it was all strictly business.

One of the mob members was an ex-army lieutenant, July Berkowitz. July was the enforcer of the mob, a violent vodka drunk that was still pissed at his country for allowing him to serve five years in a military prison for killing fourteen innocent civilians, which he did deliberately and enjoy doing so. The second mob member was DJ RIP, a local rap artist trying to make it big in the music industry and who would do whatever it took to make his dreams come true, even if that meant killing all his competition that stood in his way. Finally, the third mob member Albert Adams, a.k.a., Racist Al. Racist Al was born in Merry Hell, Mississippi. He never dated any women outside his family and wasn't friendly to anybody outside his race.

Edgar, Bugsy, and the rest of the mob members may have all different personalities, but they all loved one thing, and that was the smell of human flesh being fried on a hot skillet. So, through the grapevine, everybody that knew them around the Bronx area identified them as the Cannibal Mafia.

"Yo, motherfuckers, this casino is the best idea we had in a long time. After we ripped off those niggas at the cartel a few years back, more work has just been flowing in for us," yelled out DJ RIP as he began to puff away on his wake 'n' bake blunt. Yet he wasn't the only one feeling excited this morning. July needed to speak his mind as well.

"Fuck the cartel! We made all those fucking bitches bleed and their mothers scream. That's how we took their casino, and if anybody else gets in our way, we going to eat their wife's pussy, annihilate their stupid friends and families, and burn all their fucking houses to the ground! I'll even do it during the wintertime too, so I can spy on them from far away, watching them shake like a whore in a church in the dead blistering night! Ha, ha, ha!"

The Irish coffee was starting to kick off beautifully for their exciting morning, and as Bugsy watched the colorful fall leaves falling gradually from his opened screen window, a strange thought suddenly came upon his dreadful mind.

"In this business, gentlemen, killing another one of God's children has always been the American way, and we fitting to keep it that way too. If we want to build an empire for ourselves, then we need to do something with their bodily remains. We just can't be burying or burning them. We need to start making some money with them, so that our investments can continue to grow!"

"Yeah, great idea, Bugsy. I got two dead gooks and a black guy dead in my deep freezer back at home. We could probably start a restaurant and sell chicken-fried rice! Haha," blabbered out Racist

Al with a shit-face smile. Without even trying to be funny, he made almost everybody at the table laugh except for DJ RIP, who stood quickly to his feet quick with a angered look to his face as he stared into Racist Al's eyes and began to lay it down real thick to him about how he felt about his racial remark.

"All right, bitch! Now, I have been telling you for too many years now about your racist jokes, and if you keep talking shit, I'm going to kick you in your motherfucking head!"

"Chill out, junior! You knew what kind of guy I was before you came into this organization, and there isn't nobody twisting your arm to be here either, so if you don't like it, you can walk out that door and kick fucking rocks!"

DJ RIP's ears quickly drew back like an angry stray cat's, and without warning, he threw a left hook right across Racist Al's jaw, making him bleed from the inside of his bottom lip.

"Oh, you did it now, you little baboon. Now I won't be able to eat my favorite chili for about a week!" shouted Racist Al as he slowly rose to his feet, trying to swing back at DJ RIP. But the fight would not continue. It was quickly broken up by the rest of the guys.

"Come on, you two. Get a hold of yourselves. We can't keep playing these fucking kid games all the time with you guys," yelled Bugsy as he tried to stand tall in between the two to keep the fight from breaking out.

"You don't understand, Bugsy. I've been putting up with this fucking clown's black jokes for several years now, and I never spoke a word about it because of the respect I have for you and Mr. Edgar, but I'm speaking up now. If you don't handle his ass, then I'm going to every fucking time he gets out of line."

The frustration between DJ RIP and Racist Al was beginning to be too much for Bugsy to handle, but for those two's own sake, Bugsy had a lot of patience.

"If I got to keep doing this shit with you two, then you aren't going to fucking last long with us, and then we going to have to replace you guys, and you won't be around anymore."

"What the fuck you mean by that!" asked Racist Al.

"Oh, you know what I mean, so let's not fuck around."

After everything was said and done, the drama between the two went completely silent, and everybody went back to eating their frosted strawberry doughnuts and drinking their Irish coffee. A few minutes went by before Bugsy's cell phone finally broke the silence.

"This is Bugsy. What's up?"

"Hello, Bugsy. It's me, Mr. Finger Banger. I got your number off Edgar's phone. I'm just calling to tell you that we got some trouble down here at the hotel!"

"What kind of trouble, Finger Banger? What the fuck you talking about?"

"I found Edgar dead in his bathroom hotel about a half hour ago. I got cops down here at my hotel right now, jerking me off with all their fucking questions."

"What the fuck happened to him, Finger Banger? And why the fuck did you not call us first?"

"I'm so sorry, Bugsy. I was just scared, that's all. I wasn't for sure at the time if he was entirely dead or not, and I don't know who did this either! So you need to get your ass down here!"

"Don't snap at me, you old fucking billy goat, or I'll slap you around in front of your bitches right outside your hotel and make you look like a class-A pussy!"

"Remember, boy, who stepped upon this world first. You better show me more respect!"

"That's it, Mr. Finger Banger. We're coming down there right now, and I'm going to show you the true meaning of respect with my motherfucking fist!"

Bugsy hung up the phone and informed the rest of the mob about everything that Mr. Finger Banger had said. Sadness immediately hit all their faces, and the anger within them just wanted vengeance against anyone responsible for the death of their well-respected boss, Edgar.

FIVE

Interrogating Mr. Finger Banger

The bad news was too much for any of them to bear. Having just been informed about their dear boss's devastating tragedy, they stormed out the front door and piled into their huge black Hummer and peeled off with rage, leaving the streets swept with smoke from the small graveled rocks. With DJ RIP behind the wheel, Bugsy sitting shotgun, and the other two riding in back, loading their Uzi submachine guns, they all began speeding down the road as fast as the Hummer would go. Honking and swearing to get the other drivers to move out of their way, they were lucky to make it to the Senton Hotel without a trace of an accident. As they pulled into the parking lot of the Senton Hotel, they could see three NYPD squad cars slowly leaving from the front entrance. The four of them all began to look in every direction, looking to see if all the cops were out of sight. When it was all clear, they parked in an empty lot and pulled their ridiculous ALF masks from the inside their pockets, which they always used to hide their identities.

"Okay, everybody, listen up! The only motherfucker we must shake down here at this ragged hotel is that shit talking Mr. Finger

Banger. He said he don't know what happened to our dear friend Edgar, but I say he is lying, and we need to go in there and make his ass tell us something that we don't fucking know!" directed Bugsy. "I know where Mr. Finger Banger's office is. Me and the Boss use to come down here almost every Christmas for a great eggnog and cocaine party. You guys all just stay quiet and follow me and I'll show you the way."

They all slowly stepped out of the Hummer and shut the doors quietly to avoid bringing any attention to the Senton Hotel.

The sound of their own footsteps was all they could hear as they followed Bugsy, who led them to Mr. Finger Banger's private office. Even though Mr. Finger Banger was expecting them, Bugsy still thought it would be best if they came in a more and unusual and surprisingly way. Silence came upon them as they reached the front door to Mr. Finger Banger's office. As they put their ears up close to the door, they could hear Mr. Finger Banger on the other side, jacking off peacefully while listening to his Cyndi Lauper "She Bop" record on his antique classic Trumpet Horn Turntable. With Bugsy continuing to direct the orders, he looked to July and signaled him to bring the door down by force. With his gun already cocked back, he put the tip of the barrel just right below the doorknob so he knew he could blow the lock for sure, and within a split second, July had already unleashed several bullets in the door, leaving it in shreds. As soon as it did, Bugsy pushed July out of the way to burst through the door.

"What's up, motherfucker! Whacking-the-beaver time is over!" shouted Bugsy as he charged right toward him.

"Uh!" was the only word Mr. Finger Banger could say before Bugsy punched him with a quick lift jab, breaking his nose in one shot.

"You like talking shit on the fucking phone, don't you, you little sheep-banging monkey?" yelled Bugsy.

"Chill the fuck out, Bugsy! I was just fucking with you, really!"

"What about Edgar! What the fuck happened to him?" asked Bugsy.

"I don't know what happened to Edgar. He had already been whacked way before I did my visitor morning checks."

"What about your security cameras! Don't they work?"

"Those cameras are only for show. They are there to make the customers feel safe and secure. None of them ever worked!"

"Goddamn it, Finger Banger! You're just not telling us anything we want to hear! And because of that, I think we need to be more hostile with your ass," said Bugsy as he began to slowly take his Romanian royal dagger out from inside his right cowboy boot.

"Now, now, hold on, guys. We don't need to do this crazy shit. And why am I the only one you're fucking with? Why don't you go talk to his little grandson, George? He was the one who was supposed to pick him up here last night after he fucked that whore that he met on the fucking Live Links, and he never showed up! So, go fuck with that kid, and quit picking on a poor old man like me!" yelled Mr. Finger Banger, begging and screaming for his life to be spared.

"Where the fuck can we find grandson George and that whore? Sounds like they were the last ones to have been with him before he got whacked," asked Racist Al.

"I know where we can find George, but I don't know nothing about the whore. Maybe you can tell us more about her, Mr. Finger Banger!" said Bugsy.

"Oh, come on, you guys. I get all kinds of whores that come out to this hotel. You can't expect me to keep up with all of them. Hell, I got kids!" shouted Mr. Finger Banger.

"Don't fucking lie to us, Finger Banger. You don't have any kids, and you better tell us more about that bitch than just some stupid Live Links story!"

"Yes, I do have kids, you stupid fucking monkey! And I have a wife too. You should know, jack ass. I just sold you a porn magazine of my daughter and wife having sexual intercourse with an Australian kangaroo!"

"No shit, Mr. Finger Banger. That was a very good magazine. You say that was your family?" asked Bugsy sarcastically with a reminiscent smile.

"Yes, that was my family, you son of a bitch, and I really hope you enjoyed it, because I know I did. Ha, ha, ha."

At that moment, Bugsy had no intention of allowing Mr. Finger Banger to breathe any longer, and he let him know as much in the most profound way.

"You see, Mr. Finger Banger, we all like you, but sometimes we have to question strange shit about you. We don't know whether you coming at us in a good way or a bad way, and because of that, we feel your weirded-out, raunchy-ass penthouse hotel is no longer going to be needed in this community—which means your services will no longer be needed as well."

"Oh! Come on, you guys! I can't be that hard to figure out. I'm a fucking Gemini, for Christ's sake, and a Republican! Hey, I got it. Maybe we should bring Edgar something very special for his funeral, like some very pretty flowers and a beautiful bright red casket. The coroner gave me the business card of the funeral parlour where they took Edgar's body. I feel it would be nice if we all maybe showed up to give our dear Edgar our last respects."

But it was too late for Mr. Finger Banger. Bugsy had already made his decision upon his remaining time on earth.

"That is very thoughtful of you, Finger Banger, but unfortunately, you won't be making it, because your body won't be able, physically or mentally, to attend. Maybe spiritually, if your higher power allows you to, or even better, lets you visit your own."

"Goddamn it, Bugsy, you have always been real fucked up since the day I met you. Now, will you please just get to the fucking point? Are any of you fuck-nuts going to spare an old man's life or what?"

The last few seconds of Mr. Finger Banger's life, his body shook like a tree, and he even urinated down his own leg out of fear and frustration.

"No," Bugsy replied, and with all four men pointing their submachine guns directly at Mr. Finger Banger, they quickly opened fire, not resting until all the bullets from each of their clips were no longer of use and until his body bled out of holes in every direction. When they were finished, they watched his body drop instantly, a smile still remaining on his face, before he slowly shut his eyes and met his unfortunate death.

"Well, now that that's out of the way, what the fuck do we do now?" wondered July.

"There are four things we are going to do, gentlemen: One, take the remains, like we talked about earlier, and bring them back to the house. Two, find grandson George; maybe he knows something. Three, pay our respects to our dear friend Edgar at his funeral. Four, everybody, keep an ear out for that Live Links bitch that was with him last night; maybe she knows something too."

"You got it, Bugsy," said July and DJ RIP as they started dragging Edgar's body out of the room to put him into their Hummer. As Bugsy watched them do that, he already knew that he would be fully in charge of everything from that moment on.

"We'll find out who was responsible for the death of Edgar, and when we do, we will make sure that motherfucker pays severely and shall be executed," said Bugsy softly to himself as he reached down to pick up the funeral parlor business card that had fallen out of Mr. Finger Banger's pocket.

It read, "Dead Cheap Family Funeral Home Services, 80th St., Woodhaven, NY."

SIX

Preparing the Bodies

Watching from the review mirror, Bugsy sat on the clawed-up leather driver seat in his Hummer, overlooking the other three as they unloaded Mr. Finger Banger's body.

"Look at those guys! They look like three monkeys trying to fuck a football!" yelled Bugsy, not giving a fuck if they heard him.

"Why don't you shut the fuck up, Bugsy, and come give us a hand," replied Racist Al as he stuck his head inside the passenger window, sweating and wheezing from a brief moment of hard bloody labor.

"Yeah, that would probably be the most generous thing to do on my behalf of great leadership, but unfortunately, I got a few other errands that need attention. But don't worry. It will benefit us all!"

Without allowing Racist Al to respond, he looked at him with a Duchenne smile and drove off as fast as he could, making Racist Al wipe out and fall to the ground from being to close up to the car. As Racist Al lay down on the hard gravel rocks, all he could do was bitch and moan like a little baby as the others did nothing but laugh out loud like drunken hyenas.

"Shut the fuck *up*! All you motherfuckers shut the fuck up before I kick all your asses!"

"Man, shut the fuck up, nigga! You not going to do shit! Now get your ass up and get back to work."

So, one step after another, they all came together like a team and did what they had to do—dragging, hooking, chopping, and skinning the mangled body of Mr. Finger Banger, whatever it took to make a delicious meal for themselves.

Meanwhile driving down the street in his big black Hummer, Bugsy decided to take a cruise over at the funeral home where Mr. Edgar's body had been brought by the coroners earlier that the day.

"Eightieth St., Woodhaven, here we come. I'll just go down there and take a look-see and set up everything that needs to be done for the funeral arraignments. I got those other monkeys back at home getting dinner ready, so I won't have to get my hands dirty tonight. I have it all under control. Everything is coming together."

Bugsy may have spoken too soon, because as he arrived, he was already having second thoughts upon setting funeral arrangements with their services.

"What kind of weird out shit is this?" yelled Bugsy as he pulled up in the back parking lot behind the funeral home, where all the drug addicts and the town drag queen queers all hung out to shoot dice and needles.

"Hey, you fucking hooligans, get the fuck off the road and show some respect for the dead!" yelled Bugsy again, but the troubled street rats would not move or show any indication that they gave a flying fuck.

"We don't have to go anywhere! The streets are ours. Now drive the fuck off before I paint your truck pink and make you my bitch!" said one of the rude, stubborn drag queens as he gazed into Bugsy's eyes and began tampering with his own nipple. But Bugsy's reckless attitude was never meant to be silent, and so with rage running through his veins and his foot on the gas pedal, revving the engine over and over again, he ground his teeth and shouted out the window, "Last chance, bitches! Now, if you don't get the fuck out of this parking lot, I'm going to run all your faggot asses over with this fucking truck!"

Luckily for them, nothing had to get messy at that moment. A few coworkers from the funeral home happened to be working at the time before everybody began to flip out on each other in the middle of the parking lot.

"What the hell is going on out here?" yelled a voice from the funeral home doorway. And with wonder and rage, a man stood tall, pointing his finger at everything he saw.

"What are all of you doing out back here? This is private property. You all need to leave before I call the police!"

Right away, Bugsy knew he had to speak up before he started dialing numbers.

"Hold up, sir. You don't need to do that. I just pulled in now. I'm here to discuss funeral arrangements for a gentleman they brought in earlier today."

"What guy? What funeral arrangements? We get a lot of deadbeats that come in and out of here. You need to be more specific about who you're looking for—and what the fuck are you clowns doing back in this parking lot again? I told you before, I don't want your drag queen crack shit around here."

"It's not crack. It's heroin, you stupid fuck. Can't you tell the difference?" replied the strange drag queen.

"Look, miss … sir … I don't care what you call it … just take your junk and get the fuck out of here! I got a live customer who needs my assistance, and until you die from a slow, suffering overdose of whatever it is you endure, I frankly don't give a shit."

"I would never do my funeral services with you after I die. You guys are the absolute worst fucking funeral home on the face of the whole fucking earth!"

"Well, unfortunately, miss … sir … you have no other choice. As long as you're a part of this community in the state of New York, I am the only one your dying drug-addict ass could possibly afford. So, on more shorter terms, miss … sir … when you die, your ass belongs to me. Now, for the second time, get the fuck out of here!"

Without any other words to say, the strange drag queen and his ragged drug-addict friends quickly grabbed all their belongings and pushed in another direction.

"Sorry about all that commotion that you had to witness. I know you're probably going through some difficult times right now and this is the last shit you want to pile on your plate. My name is Robert, but everybody calls me the Corpse Bandit, and I'll be your funeral home director. Now, what can I do for you?"

The negative energy within Robert began to dissolve, and Bugsy rapidly felt relieved that he could now talk to him like a normal person without any desire to kick his ass.

"The name is Bugsy. I was told that the corpse of a Mr. Edgar would be here at this funeral parlor. I would like to view the body and set up funeral arrangements immediately. A lot of his friends and family would sure like to attend."

"Where in the fuck is the family at? Don't they know that he is deceased?" Robert pondered.

"Well, not exactly Mr. Corpse Bandit. I had a few errands I had to run today, but I am definitely going to disclose that to them as soon as possible—I promise you that," said Bugsy with a smug, smirking face.

"Hey, goddamn it! I run a serious business here, and I expect you to take this matter seriously as well. Now, please step into my office so we can handle these sudden circumstances."

With a pressing look on Bugsy's face, he softly stepped into the doorway, saying nothing at all.

"Okay, Bugsy, just letting you know right now that in this procedure, there are three steps that I will walk you through. Number one, I'll show you Mr. Edgar and arrange the proper clothing for his body. Number two would be choosing a casket that you think would be satisfying to his liking. And three is my favorite: tombstone design. Please, don't ask questions about the price at this moment. I'm telling you right now, Bugsy, there will be one, and we will need someone to look after these financial matters as well. So, Bugsy, are you still wanting to ally with us here at our beloved family funeral home?"

Bugsy didn't have to give too much thought to this; he didn't have too much time anyway, and he didn't feel like going from one funeral home to another just to look for the perfect place.

"This place is going to do just fine, Mr. Corpse Bandit. Hell, I would bring my momma here if I hadn't thrown her over the Grand Canyon a few years back."

"Wow, man! That must have been exciting. I bet you could hear that bitch's dying screams falling a hundred miles down."

"Yes, Mr. Corpse Bandit, it will always be a sweet, warm, and memorable moment in my life. I always had family problems growing up. Another black sheep with mental disorders."

"Nah, don't be so hard on yourself. I'm sure you had your reasons, just like I did when I killed my mother. Except I fed her to the hyenas down in the Congo Basin, Africa. Told her I wanted to give her something very … special for Mother's Day, and I sure did too. Haha. Never saw it coming."

Just talking to Robert for a few brief minutes made Bugsy feel right at home, and with all that being set aside, Robert even introduced Bugsy to the rest of his staff to make him feel more comfortable about who would be preparing the body of his dear beloved boss and friend, Mr. Edgar.

"I would like to introduce another my staff members, who oversees the preparation downstairs in our embalming room. His name is Mr. Cat Litter, but everyone knows him as Drunken Randy, because he likes to pass out! During the cremation of bodies, he almost burned the fucking place down twice, didn't you, Randy?"

And all Drunken Randy could do was sit there with a shamed look on his face, as if he couldn't be more embarrassed.

"And last but not least is good old Ernest. Ernest is our tombstone designer. He got an IQ of a high 55 and is on his way to a great clown school university after he graduates high school."

"How old is he?" wondered Bugsy.

"He's almost thirty-five years old, but don't let the age fool you. This used-to-be kid is pure fucking genius."

The four of them looked at each other with psychotic smiles and said no more as the shiny black pin and the folded-up, wrinkled contract came out of Mr. Corpse Bandit's inside coat pocket. Bugsy never cared to overlook the contract. The impatient, stubborn mule that he always was, he signed without a thought in his mind. The others stood still and tall as they looked at each other, looking skeptical as fuck as they all watched and laughed. It was as if Bugsy was signing his life away or something. But to Bugsy, it was just a stupid funeral home contract. It wasn't like he was getting married or something. And so, after the T's were crossed and the I's were dotted, they all shook hands and began to walk Bugsy directly out the back door. They stood together and waved him off as he slowly drove away in his big black Hummer. Looking at his watch, he began to speed down the road, realizing had been gone for a little longer than he thought. He also realized the funeral home staff never ran him through the three-step procedure, like they said they would.

"Nah, they will pick everything out beautifully, and it will all be fine," he said to himself with no worries whatsoever. And so, he continued to drive down the road, trying to take every shortcut possible to make it home safe and sound with the others so he could feed his growling stomach, which had been bothering him for the past hour.

"Goddamn pedestrians always walking on the fucking sidewalk. Get the fuck out the way!" Bugsy yelled as he literally began to cut through street corners, trying his best not to hit anybody on his way home. But as his stomach continued to growl, he grew even more impatient, and by the time he pulled up to the front of the house, he was reckless and mad and didn't have any desire to speak a word to anyone. His only ambition at that moment was to eat a lot of food and smoke a lot of weed. Hopefully, he could pass out so he could master-plan everything that needed to be done for tomorrow. But as he heard the loud music playing from outside the house as he stepped out of the truck, he realized the rest of the guys had already started a little party of their own. That might just break the ice a little and settle his short temper.

Wiping his feet on the "NO JEWS ALLOWED" doormat that Racist Al had gotten them all for Christmas last year, Bugsy quickly turned the knob on the splintered door handle and stepped right in to inform everybody, so gladly, that he was home.

"Hey, hey, you stupid fucking monkeys!" shouted Bugsy with joy, hoping everybody would hear him. But they didn't. The music was too loud, and they were all in the kitchen, just about ready to eat their home-cooked meal, which they called Finger Banger tenderloins.

"I said hey, you stupid fucking monkeys, I'm home!" Bugsy said once again as he peeked his head through the kitchen door.

"Oh, hey, Bugsy. Nice to see you're finally home. Please join us for dinner. It's hot and ready," said July with greasy BBQ blood dripping down from the bottom of his lip.

"Oh, fuck yeah! This all looks so good!"

"Yeah, it tastes good too, nigga. I marinated this motherfucker in my special sauce myself."

"Thank you RIP. It has always been a great pleasure working with you," replied Bugsy as he began to dig his teeth into his juicy, fatty, bloody tenderloin.

"So, where did you drive off to again?" wondered July.

"I found the place where Edgar's body is being held, so I made funeral arrangements and left. But we still need to talk to grandson George, see if he knows anything, and keep a look out for that stupid Live Links bitch."

Still, the question about the funeral home was genuinely on July's mind.

"So, tell us more about the funeral home. Is it a hole in the wall or what? Did you even get to see Edgar's body? Is he all fucked up? What about the funeral? What time and day is that?"

"Jesus fucking Christ, man! Everything is being handled by the beautiful established Dead Cheap Family Funeral Home Services. They will call us when they are ready, so please, no more fucking questions from anybody, okay! Boss Edgar is dead, and there isn't a damn thing we can do about it but pay our respects and kill the motherfucker that did it."

"We don't even know who the fuck did it," blabbered DJ RIP.

"Listen up, fellas, I'm hurting just as bad as all of you are. Because of this motherfucker, our dream to run our first casino no longer exists. But I tell you all one thing, and quote me on this if you like: I promise you all, from the bottom of my heart, we are going to find this asshole, even if it takes the death of me. We will find this motherfucker. Believe in me, and I'll guide you all the way."

There was no doubt in any of the other men's minds. They all felt the inspiration in the air and knew they could trust in Bugsy to find who was reasonable for the death of their boss, Edgar.

"Well, my great grandfather, Waylon Frederick Marshall, was a well-known slave owner way back in the seventeen hundreds, down in the state of Mississippi. My daddy always told me growing up that he never had too many slaves running away, because they were always scared shitless, and even when they did try to make a run for it, my grandfather would always drag their black asses right back. And so, that's how I know I have it in my blood to find this fucking guy."

Nobody really found too much sense in Racist Al's unearthly statement, especially DJ RIP, but Bugsy knew he had to accept the love and bring them all in together.

"That's the spirit, guys. If we all come together as a team, we can find this motherfucker and bring him to our own brand of justice. But for now, let's go pay grandson George a visit."

SEVEN
Fucking Shit Up

After about an hour of grinding down on their delicious, homemade human remains, a cold bottle of Montoya Cabernet red wine awaited them in their rusted old ice chest freezer.

"I know you all could use something cold to wash this shit down with," yelled DJ RIP as he got up quickly to bust out the bottle from the freezer.

"All right, all you niggas get a glass and pour yourself a drink so we can have a toast before we head out to our mission—and that means you too, Racist Al, you little babbling bitch! Now, we all know what we need to do. Therefore, we don't need to go over this shit again. Because if I have to, I'll take a crowbar to each and every one of your motherfucking heads! Starting with yours, Racist Al. So, in other words, let's be professional out there and understand our true value as the psychotic fucks we are so we can all prosper in our absurd future that lies ahead of us. Cheers!"

All four men raised their stolen A&W Root Beer glasses to the air, wishing they were actually real wine glasses, then hit their glasses together with a echoing bang that bounced off the wall, and took a drink with their devilish smiles as they finished their wine in seconds and asked for another. After they had drink the last drips of their finest Montoya Cabernet red wine bottle, Bugsy threw it against the wall. He picked up the shattered pieces from the bloodstained kitchen floor as they all slowly walked out of the house to fulfill their mission of tracking down grandson George and finding more word about the Live Links bitch they had heard around so much but knew so little about. Pushing each other out of the way as they piled into the Hummer, with Bugsy behind the wheel, he started the car and began to slowly drive away without any signs of his old road rage behavior.

Debating which street or route would be best to catch grandson George, he knew his grandfather's old classic Hotchkiss Limousine shouldn't be too hard to find, given that it stuck out like a sore thumb. But Bugsy knew the cat-and-mouse game would soon die out and they would need to invade homes immediately, starting with George's parents' house. But at the same time, Bugsy had no information about where they lived; the only one who did was George's grandmother, Edger's wife, Dorothy, a wife who still didn't know that her husband, Edgar, had been killed the other night. Now Bugsy felt dishonored and irritated that he would have to break the news to her.

"God fucking damn it, man! I'm not trying to have no crying, slobbering bitch all up in my arms at this time. So now I got to tell this bitch that her husband's dead and we need to know where her grandson is at so we can kick his ass! This is going to be a long night!"

As DJ RIP and Racist Al looked to the ground and slowly shook their heads, only July offered a possible suggestion.

"Look here, Bugsy. I dealt with these types of emotional problems with people before, and I felt I might just know how to break it down to Edgar's wife better then you can. So, if you don't mind, I would love to do the honors while the rest of you search the house and find out where grandson George's parents live."

Bugsy felt truly relieved that July was willing to go through with all the depressing and heartbreaking moments with Edgar's wife, Dorothy.

"Oh, boy! Do you really mean that? That sure would be a burden off my shoulders. I can't wait to get started. Come on, let's get to their house!" yelled Bugsy with a smile on his face. He put his foot down on the gas and began to speed recklessly down the road without a care in the world.

"Everything is going to be fine, boys! Everything is going to be fine," said Bugsy out loud as he began to flip through his brand-new six-disc car stereo that he pilfered off a shelf at a rundown K-Mart store.

"Oh, shit here's an album I haven't heard in a long time. Some good old-fashion Creedence Clearwater Revival! Now, if none of you motherfuckers haven't heard these guys, then I don't know whose pussy you popped out of, but I tell you one thing. They better put you back in if you don't know, because you're not ready for this world quite yet."

He sang loudly and clapped his hands together all the way to George's grandmother's house. The others quickly grew annoyed and could not wait to finally arrive so they could be free from Bugsy's irritating singing voice.

"Hey, Bugsy, you think you could drive this motherfucker any faster? My stomach is not felling very well. I must have ate too much or something," yelled DJ RIP as he began rubbing his stomach firmly while his eyes slowly rolled back towards the sky. But the others didn't pay too much attention, as if they thought it was more than just eating way too much. As if maybe they thought he had a fever and they didn't want to catch his perilous contagious disease. So they all kept their distance and opened all their windows, just in case he needed to quickly vomit over something, so it wouldn't be all over them.

"Don't you worry RIP, we are almost there! If I know Edgar's wife, 1 know that bitch will have some kind of cheap vodka and tomato juice. We can make you a quick Bloody Mary. That always makes my stomach feel much better when its turned upside down."

"That boy don't drink no goddamn Bloody Mary. You going to have to pour him a warm-piss bottle of 40 oz. malt liquor! Or maybe even some Kool-Aid, isn't that right, DJ RIP?"

The ungracious humor in Racist Al's statement did nothing but rapidly anger DJ RIP.

"You better shut the fuck up, Racist Al, before I knock all your motherfucking teeth down your motherfucking throat!" replied DJ RIP, as he began sweating his sickness all down his face, trying his best not to brush up against anything until he got to the house, where he could then ask for a clean, cold towel, hoping that he could put his own indisposed ass at ease. Watching Rip wiping the sweat off his forehead with his right jack-off hand made everyone feel even more worried during their trip to Grandmother Dorothy's house.

"The fuck you all looking at? We almost there anyway, so quit looking so fucking heedful! Goddamn, you all are like a barrel of fucking observing monkeys. What are you, the FBI or something? All right, everybody shut the fuck up! We are pulling up the driveway right now!" yelled Bugsy. The rest of the guys tried standing up, suddenly bumping their heads on the ceiling in the inside of the truck, as they were so eager to leave.

"Okay, bitches, now get the fuck out of my car. I'm tired of babysitting you little queer-bait faggots!"

As they all stepped out of the big black Hummer to stretch their arms and legs, they quickly noticed the strangest little things about the grandmother's house, things they would never forget until they were dead in the ground or in some lonely ditch. But on the bright side, the sun was almost down when they arrived, and it was nearly blinding their eyes as they looked at the habitation they were about to enter. The house was bright and pink, like a 1950s flashback, and there was a white picket fence on each side of the house, with warning signs that read nothing but baffling shit such as,

Death is among us.
No crazy drama ladies allowed.
No humping goats without a rubber.
Don't share used needles.
Always be the first motherfucker to do it.

Last and least was a Ty Cobb photo, nailed to the front door, that read,

Don't come home a failure.

Everything about the place was unusual to everyone except Bugsy. He really seemed to like it a lot.

"Don't worry, boys. Like I said before, everything is going to be fine!"

They all slowly followed behind Bugsy as he made his way mercifully toward the front door. And with his head held high and a more serious mourning look upon his face, he reached for the golden Scrooge door knocker and began knocking firmly away. With just a slight look over his left shoulder, he saw July diagonally right behind him, and with a single quick gesture, he quickly grasped July by his arm and pulled him promptly next to him to wrathfully whisper into his left ear, "Now, look here! Your job is to break the unpleasant news to this half-dying woman in the most unperturbed manner and without giving this ramshackle bitch a heart attack. Be nice and be calm! Me and the rest of the fellas will introduce ourselves peaceable and then carefully dig up as much information as possible without giving Grandmother Dorothy a scant bit of distress over what we're doing. Tell her a story about a loss loved one in your life. Old people love stories. It makes them feel right at home, like an after-hour bingo party without any annoying grandkids asking stupid questions. Don't agonize yourself, and remember, this was your fucking idea! So you're not backing out of this bitch, you got that? Now, look pleasant before she answers the door. I don't want her to think that you're some creepy homosexual salesman!"

They all stood there waiting peacefully, as the could hear Grandmother Dorothy's footsteps coming closer to the door. Wondering what kind of character she would be, all they could do was hope for a stable-minded person.

"I'm coming! I'm coming!" she hollered with a screeching elderly voice. As they began to watch the door knob turn so slightly, all their hearts began to race in a joyfully curious way, to the point where thought they might have to hold their laughter under their breath, if she appeared in some ridiculous manner.

"Hey there, gentlemen, what can I do for you? Please don't take too much of my time. I have an urgent diarrhea problem, and I'm not trying to let all the mosquitoes in the house cause of talking to you dumb fucks!"

After her short, sincere statement, July looked into her eyes and began to tell her everything.

"Hello, miss. How you doing this evening? My name is July, and these are my sidekick halfwit friends that are tagging along with me today. I'm afraid I have very heartbreaking news to inform you about. A huge tragedy occurred the other night. Your husband, Edgar, was involved, and I'm not sure yet quite how to break it to you."

Right away, Grandmother Dorothy assumed her husband Edgar was in trouble with the law, like the scandalmonger he always was. Without even giving a thought, she jumped to conclusions right away.

"If that bastard winds up in jail again, then it isn't any heartbreaking news. You can tell him to keep his ass there overnight, 'cause I'm not going to pay out of my purse to get him out!"

"No, miss. I'm afraid this situation is a little more complicated than that."

"What the fuck are you talking about, sir? I don't even know you. The only moron I unfortunately know out of your halfwit group is that little puss-wad right there. Bugsy! The one who I always caught stealing vodka out of my liquor cabinet whenever Edgar and I were busy playing cards with next-door neighbors. What's the matter, Bugsy? Were you hoping I wouldn't recognize you? Is that why you got this other dipshit doing all the talking, because you're not man enough to do it yourself?"

The slick and clever man that Bugsy always thought he was, he made sure he always had an answer for every question that was asked.

"No, not at all, miss. I just thought that maybe—"

But Bugsy couldn't even finish his sentence. Grandmother Dorothy felt she had a more urgent issue that needed to be corrected.

"I am a married women, you fucking idiot! It's not miss! Its missus! My name is Mrs. Nut Stain! Why is that so hard for you to remember? Nobody else I know has a problem remembering that. It's an old, classy name that a king would give his royal whore daughter after she would give her first hand job to a drunken Jester many years ago. The fucking name is golden! And don't forget the missus part again, or else I'll beat the shit out of you with my ring finger! No, what is it you all want? I'm not going to stand out here all day and night.

It was on the tip of Bugsy's tongue to bring up the death of her husband, Edgar. But luckily for his sake, July stepped in to keep his promise, for which he volunteered. And so, without wasting any more valuable time, he quickly proceeded with the devastating news.

"If you don't mind, Mrs. Nut Stain, I would like for us to both sit down for what I'm about to say. Because I know you're not going to like or believe what is about to come out of my mouth. I wish I had something more delightful to share with you this evening, but unfortunately, in this case, there really isn't."

Mrs. Nut Stain didn't know exactly how take the serious look on July's face. It was as if there were a dark cloud slowly drifting over her tree of life. She began to believe there truly was a troubling matter about her beloved husband, Edgar.

"Oh, dear. My darling Edgar. What have you done now?" she said to herself, utterly dispirited. And as she looked directly into the sky, she began to pray heavily, without breaking her concentration, hoping for the best outcome of the breaking news before she welcomed her unexpected visitors into her unusual home.

"Will you please come in gentlemen, and don't forget to wipe your feet on the mat. I didn't have too much time to pick up the place today, but just try to make yourself at home and find a place to sit. I'll be over in the kitchen fetching something comforting to snack on and a little something souped up to drink."

The men felt vastly relieved that the stubborn old bitch was finally going to let them in so they could be on their way of taking care of the drastic dying drama and grasping any information about grandson George's home address. Right away, July could tell just by looking around the house that there was nobody else in the home other than Mrs. Nut Stain. And being the great soldier that July once was, he quickly began to conduct himself like one as well.

"Okay, gentlemen. First things first. We need to get medical attention for our friend here, DJ RIP, so he can be a more helpful for us. And me and Mr. Bugsy will occupy Mrs. Nut Stain with our supportive psychological intelligence."

Racist Al, without a direct order, began to feel unaccounted for, and within a blink of an eye, he was at the boiling point and ready to fight.

"*Hey*, you dumb fucking Cub Scout! Are you just going to jerk their dicks all day, or are you going to give me some loving too? Don't leave me out, motherfucker! I have tremendously soft feelings, and I don't like when people make me feel unappreciated. I have been walking on this world too long, and I'm going to get the true amount of respect that I know my perfectionist ass deserves. You understand me, you little walking-tall wannabe badass. I should kick your ass right now and teabag your pretty-boy face just to watch you cry like a bitch."

The furious beast within July made him feel extremely eager to strangle Racist Al at that moment. But with so much at stake, he had no other choice but to draw back and be the better man. Although that wouldn't have been his normal decision, being the kind of lunatic he was, still, he felt there was no need for the dispute to continue any further.

"Hey, man, please keep your voice down. We can't be doing this shit right now. There is an abnormal elderly bitch back in the kitchen about to take in some serious mental emotions in the next minute or two, and I need you to be more coolheaded. You're my friend, Al, and I love you like a brother. So, let's please not throw that friendship away on just another miserable day in life."

The limited amount of time that July put into his vast and smooth discussion with Racist Al, which he thought he had laid down so beautiful and thick, still was not enough to cool things over, and so, without giving it a bit of thought, Racist Al struck back again, fighting fire with fire, so he could fulfill some emotional needs of his own.

"You were never a friend. You just thought it would be so fucking righteous to befriend a lonely guy like me. You just wanted to be nice—that's all! Well, let me tell you something, buddy boy! I don't like fucking nice guys who try to be fucking nice just because he feels like it's the right thing to do. That shit sickens me. It makes me think that you're less than a man in every kind of way, boy! It makes me think you got no heart and everything about you is a lie. It makes me think there is no truth in your soul and your mommy and daddy raised a fucking sheep puppet. Now, how does that make you feel, little man?"

The tension in the room was becoming serious. Both men were now on the same demented page of wanting to annihilate the other, and nobody had any desire to play referee. With DJ RIP avoiding the conflict to look after the medical needs of his upset stomach, Bugsy just stood there with a jolly attitude, clapping and cheering away as July and Racist Al continued their immoral ways.

"Don't call me little man, Al! I'm a bigger beast than you are, and you know it! And so does your whore cousin that you have been fucking for the past ten years of your pathetic life. And let me tell you one more thing. For a gap-toothed, bushy redhead, she sure can suck a good dick with that pretty crooked mouth and those beautiful, blistering, cheery lumps on her lips. Now, how does that make you feel, you muttering little bitch?"

Racist Al couldn't believe what he had just heard, and the stench of jealousy flew swiftly in the air, sending Racist Al into a madness of rage. He swung at Bugsy with his fist just like the Southern rebel he always was.

"You son of a bitch! Those cheery, lump lumpy lips were my favorite part of that old skank dog! Now I'm going to wring your fucking neck!"

As the fight broke out, Bugsy quickly moved out the way and yelled for DJ RIP to come over and enjoy the horrific live main event that he was ring mastering in the middle of Mrs. Nut Stain's living room.

"Yo, Bugsy, man, what the fuck are all you dumb-ass niggas doing? This old lady is about to start flipping out if she sees all this shit!"

"So what? Fuck that bitch! We were going to kill her anyway. As a matter of fact, why don't you go now into the kitchen and take this here old sailor knife and slice her fucking throat! I'm trying to conduct business here."

Bugsy handed DJ RIP the knife and continued to host the fright show of the night between July and Racist Al. But the dreadful idea of slicing Mrs. Nut Stain's throat was the absolute last thing on RIP's mind, and without any thought of trying to persuade Bugsy from killing Mrs. Nut Stain, he just buckled up and did it. The earth then began to revolve for RIP as he began to walk slowly toward the kitchen door, and just like any true killer's heart, his began beating more rapidly than anyone else's on the face of the fucking planet.

There was no turning back for DJ RIP, as he was face to face with the kitchen door. With just one look to the sky, to asked his Lord and Savior for his blessing. He then quickly made his way right through the entrance. As soon as he walked in, he was prepared not to startle her in any kind of way. She was still digging in the fridge for those comforting snacks that she was nice enough to offer her unexpected guess. And so, with the sailor knife that Bugsy had given him, he quickly got her undivided attention by clearing his throat. Her head shot up like a rocket launching to the moon. The second she saw RIP standing there, motionless, looking deep into her eyes as his hand clutched hard on the beat-up old sailor knife, she broke into tears, leaving her heart no other option but to give in to discomposure as her mind pondered in a confused, petrified manner, "What is this? What's going on?"

She stuttered in panic as the glass jar of mayonnaise slipped from her sweating palms and shattered all over the hard tile. With no remorse, DJ RIP stepped into striking zone and punctured a slight deep gash upon Mrs. Nut Stain's right cheekbone, and without any goodhearted disposition, he rapidly began to do it repeatedly as he watched her screaming fearfully for her life, hoping the neighbors could not hear a single solitary word.

"Oh, my God! Why is this happing to me?" she screamed as her legs began shaking nervously, making her fall flat to the ground.

From that moment on, DJ RIP knew there was no need for any more engagement with the old sailor knife, as he now saw Mrs. Nut Stain's body being sent into shock from all the traumatic torture he had set upon her. Watching Mrs. Nut Stain breathing heavily as he stood next to her, staring down with a significant look, he then began to speak to inform her everything about her husband Edgar's situation.

"Listen up, bitch! I know you can hear me, and I'm only going to say this once. Your husband is dead. He was murdered last night. We don't know who it was, but we are trying to find out. Now, if you can just kindly tell me where I can find your grandson George, I promise you I'll gladly doctor you up myself instead of leaving you here to die an old, worthless, dried-up Jezebel."

Meanwhile, on the other side of the wall, in the now wreck and ruin living room, Racist Al and July's wildly and unnecessary behavior was still taking place, and Bugsy was still hosting as some deranged ringmaster, which he had created in his own clever mind just so he could continue the roughhousing brawl between the two idiots who would not bury the hatchet anytime soon. But just like every fight, there is always a winner and a loser. And in this fight, the victor's luck was falling at long last into July's lap, leaving Racist Al with heavy arms and short of breath. Finally, July grabbed him by the collar of his coat and flung him in through the kitchen wall, making DJ RIP jump to his feet at spring force, as Mrs. Nut Stain could do nothing but look up with a small gesture of her head.

"Goddamn, man, what the fuck are all you motherfuckers doing?" shouted DJ RIP in a surprisingly panicked way. Racist Al slowly got up from his fall and began dusting drywall crumbs off each shoulder. The long and viciously pointless fight had at last come to a sudden stop with the help of DJ RIP and Bugsy's lousy arbiter performance.

"Okay, you two, enough is enough! We fucked shit up good already. I think it's time for us to push on and torch this house down to smoke and ashes," shouted RIP angrily as he came between the two, trying his best to make them shake hands by force. But the two wouldn't budge, and Bugsy had to step in quickly to play the comical asshole that he sometimes loved to be.

"That was one hell of a show, you two crazy motherfuckers! Woo! I would absolutely pay to see that again. But for right now, we should probably all get the fuck out of here and collect what we need. Now, what do we have here? You still haven't killed this bitch yet, RIP?"

"We still need get this bitch to give us the answers that we need to find grandson George!"

Once again, July stepped in to quickly volunteer.

"Don't you all worry about a fucking thing. Start pouring gas all over the house, and prepare for it to be burned down into little pieces. I'll just need one minute with this bitch to make her tell me everything we need to know."

As everyone cleared the room, the sudden silence of pessimistic energy began to overtake Mr. Nut Stain's demented mind. The only thing left for July to do at that moment was to force Mrs. Nut Stain to spit out all information that was needed and to get that information by any means necessary. With now only July and Mrs. Nut Stain in the small demolished kitchen, July began to talk to Mrs. Nut Stain in his most calm and gentle way.

"This unexpected disaster that we brought to you today must be extremely terrifying for you. I don't know if you were told or not, but your husband's dead, and we are trying to find the motherfucker that did it. But for us to figure out that, we're going to need to know where we can find your grandson George. Now, do you think you can help us out with that?"

Mrs. Nut Stain seemed very mad and confused, as if she were wondering why things had to turn out this way for such a poor cause.

"That was the fucking information that you all needed from me? Why didn't you fuckheads just come direct from the start. I would have given you his address! I don't even like that little fucker all that much anyway!"

All July could do at that moment was look to the ceiling, feeling nothing but absolute senselessness and frustration. Still, even though Mrs. Nut Stain had showed her true emotions about the situation,

July's thoughts about killing her were still in effect. So now, as Mrs. Nut Stain lay on the hard, cold kitchen floor, asking and hoping for July to spare her life and reach for her Life Alert neckless, which was hiding under the greasy stove, July made his decision and avoided her request so he could share with her a brief story about life and death in his own foul way.

"Please, don't take this horrible night too seriously. People die every day. Some die alone in a tormented hospital. Some die amongst others inside a burning church. And some die in a puddle of blood under the blistering sun in the Registan desert. About six years back, I was a lieutenant for the United States Army. I had just turned twenty-seven, and they had just sent me out to my first duty called, Operation Haven Denial. About forty-five miles outside Kandahar, Afghanistan, there was an unsuspecting road bomb that exploded enormously, leaving six men dead at the blast site within seconds.

"The sounds of civilians screaming and M240 machine guns were roaring everywhere, and my duty was to obtain the wounded and direct all civilians to safety. And I did just that. This safe place was somewhere where nobody could find them and where nobody could hear them. The place that came to mind was a small Tora Bora cave located inside the Spin Ghar Mountains. My worthwhile luck couldn't have come at a better time. The ones I secured were a family of three—father, mother, and daughter. They were so grateful to have been saved by a wonderful, caring soldier. It's just too bad they didn't know that I was the absolute opposite of wonderful and caring and that I had no desire to keep them around any longer. My disturbed patriotic mind was overcrowded with bizarre ideas, and I couldn't wait to unleash them. It wasn't hard for me to part them from each other violently because I use to work at a child protective services office, and they would always force me to do all the dirty work. It would always be an honor watching a little kid cry and be carried away by some unknown stranger they had never seen before. Even though, most of the time, that stranger was me, and they were never seen again. But anyway, back to the story. As I stood there debating which one of the three I should kill first, I knew it would be best to take out the male of the species so I could leave the mother and daughter in a more panicked situation. I didn't need to do anything special with the old man, so I just fucking shot him in the throat, leaving his blood dripping slowly all over the back of the wall as his family screamed in distress. I didn't think too much of it after it was done, so I quickly snatched the little girl from her mother's filthy sticky hands and began to carve her eye out with a pointed gravel rock that was lying near me on the ground. The kid was a pussy! She couldn't take the pain, and so, just like the father, I also had no use for her. So, without allowing her mom to kiss her goodbye on her pretty little cheek, that her dark brown eyeball was dangling off, I soundly put her to death with hand-over-mouth suffocation, leaving only the mother now, all by her lonesome. Her beauty quickly aroused me, but I knew a great sexual encounter would be a lot more uplifting if her body was deceased and ready for me to fuck! And so, without any questions asked, I forced her to put those same old filthy and sticky hands down my GI fatigues and jerk me off repeatedly until she could wash those filthy and sticky hands with my creamy cleansing cum. *You* should have saw the look on this bitch's face, Mrs. Nut Stain, because you remind me a lot of her."

July's long-lasting story was beginning to irritate Mrs. Nut Stain, and she wasn't sure if she could bear hearing any more of his pointless and demented tale.

"Hey, asshole! Are you done telling your fucking story yet? I'm another victim dying on this cold floor. You can kill me any time you want so I won't have to listen to any more of your sick and twisted shit!"

With Mrs. Nut Stain being dispassionate, still gashing blood from her disfigured face from RIP's earlier brutal outburst, and the other guys waiting outside as they misbehaved childishly in the Hummer, honking the horn repeatedly, yelling for July to hurry up and finish everything from inside, he had no choice but to cut the story short and kill her off quickly.

"Goddamn it! I can never leave a crime scene on good terms!" he cried out loud as he began to look around for a death-dealing object to finish off her long-awaited death.

"Oh, shit! Look at what we got here. An old greased-up frying pan, just waiting to be used to bash an old lady's cranky fucking head in."

A huge Grinch smile came upon Mrs. Nut Stain's face as he said those magical words to her low-budget hearing aids, and as she lay there on her back, looking up at July holding the frying pan so tightly in his hands, he began to strike away at her head, bashing it over and over again until he could see her brains pop out from the side and she can no longer breath.

"My work is now done here!" he said to himself as he looked down on her blood-soaked corpse. And with just a slight look out of corner of his eye, he spotted a black leather book sitting peacefully under the microwave. A black book that read, "Directory" on the front cover and held all the phone numbers and addresses to everyone she knew, including her own grandson George. So now, having the information that they needed, he scooped up the book, and with nothing left to do but go ahead with the finale, he flipped out a match and smelled the stench of gasoline that was smothering the room so heavily. Finally, he burned it down, leaving the house in smoky, fiery flames as he slowly walked out the door to smell the glorious air in the dark, gloomy night.

EIGHT
Just Another Victim

The flames grew higher and higher as the smoke drifted throughout the house, forcing the windows to overheat, shattering into pieces, the smoke beginning to glide throughout every inch of the home, squeezing through the cracks to flee into the dark blue sky. A crowd of people watched with big shocked eyes throughout the entire neighborhood, and without a thought of calling the police, they just stood there and gossiped about hair appointments, football games, and how to strangle a racehorse if it came in last place. But wondering how the fire started never came to mind as they all gathered around to appreciate a peacefully laid-out bonfire. Their mouths began to drool as an old drunken homeless guy pulled out a big bag of marshmallows from his old high school book bag, which he still had from the day he dropped out years ago.

Watching the house falling to its fiery death as they slowly drove away, the four of them began to laugh and cheer, filled with hope of finding the one who was responsible for the murder of their boss. Having the big black directory book at that very moment was like having the keys to the world. Without any more questions, they circled grandson George's address with a worn-out pen and began to navigate away as Bugsy continued driving down the road.

"We got this motherfucker now! So, let's go knock over his house, fuck his mother, and smack his ass around a little bit until he tells us what we need to know," shouted Bugsy at the top of his lungs. Once again, great luck had come out of nowhere and fallen into their lap, because from just about a half a mile up, Bugsy unexpectedly spotted Edgar's old Hotchkiss limousine, dining at an adult film drive-through theater, with grandson George and his obese girlfriend inside, holding hands and touching tongues.

"There he goes! Right over at the Stink 'N' the Pink Theater. Come on, fellas, let's go break up his rated-G playdate and beat the living shit out of him!"

The Stink 'N' the Pink Adult Film Theater was on a busy street where everybody could drive by and see it shining like a burning star. You couldn't miss something so sexually explicit and disturbing to the public community. A fifty-foot-tall billboard that revealed some of the movies that were playing that night shimmered brightly with purple neon lights over all the corrupted and perverted regulars and newcomers entering and exiting the crumbling old theater. *Snow White and Her Drunk And Horny Dwarfs*, *Cat Woman Does Wonder-Woman, Volume 2*, *How the Grinch Stole a Bitch's Virginity*, and, of course, the movie that the two little lovebirds were sitting together and so peacefully watching in their Hotchkiss Limousine: *The Bestiality Nightlife of Beauty and the Beast*.

It was an exceptionally romantic evening for just the two of them, and there was no keeping them apart, unless it involved drugs, money, or a plate of food. Or in this case, being abducted and tormented by Bugsy and his mob. There wasn't too much to think about when it came to snatching George out of his car. The deviants within the crowed were too occupied watching their whacked-out films and fulfilling their need for pleasure with self-stimulation, so now, only moments away from having George in their custody, they put their ALF masks on once again and began to pace quickly across the street, to the Stink 'N' the Pink Theater. Creeps, weirdos, and drag

queens were lurking everywhere and stopping them to say hello, just
so they could take a few moments to undress them with their crack-
addict eyes. And as they got ready to burst through the security guard
at the front gate, they all took out their personal handguns from their
back pockets and rushed in quietly and politely. Bugsy led the way.
He did most of the talking as well.

"Please don't say a fucking word, Mr. Security man. We are just
here to scoop up a young gentleman, and we will be out of your hair
in no time. And because we worry about your financial income, we
have a little endorsement of our own. And so, without any loud noise
out of your mouth or any attempts of alerting authority, we will be
happy to share with you a thousand dollars for your troubles, to keep
nice and quiet for the next few minutes. Now, do you think you can
handle that?"

There was no sign of hesitation upon the security officer's. It was
as if he had been involved in more gunpoint situations than they all
thought. There also were no signs of him being a righteous hero or,
God forbid, an ex-cop. Bugsy felt that he was too mistrustful looking
for that. His unworried, coolheaded attitude was beginning to piss
off Bugsy and his mob, and the security officer felt that energy right
away and knew that it would be best to speak up about his thoughts,
specifically about their grateful offer of a thousand dollars.

"There is no need for your guns, gentlemen. I'm a peaceful man.
And there is no need for your masks either, because the only cameras
working in this place are in the ladies' restroom. I would know because
I installed them myself, and I don't plan on taking them down. Now,
to answer to your question regarding the thousand dollars. I'm sorry,
fellas, but I'm going to have to turn that down and make you all give
me something worth more worth my while."

The ALF masks, which they always wore so proudly over their
faces, finally came off slowly with a tug of their hands. By the looks
of all their eyes, they were getting impatient with the security officer's
unknown needs.

"You should have taken took the money, Mr. Security Man,

because the only thing we can give you that's going to be more worth your while is your own valuable life, you greedy little fuck!"

Once again, the look of a brilliant weasel came upon his face, and with no worry at all, he responded with some turned-over troubling news.

"You see, fellas, that's where you're wrong! First of all, I'm a degenerate suicidal with nothing else to do with my life but jack myself off or die! That's why I took this job. If you kill me right now, you would only be doing me a favor. Second of all, if I push this alarm here, then every cop in New York City will show up, because they know how much their precious after-hour jack-off theater means to them. Fucking with me is like fucking with every New Yorker's right to masturbate. And that right there, buddy, is like playing with fire at an oil-spill contest."

Bugsy didn't feel like going down that road, and so, with a slow, overly irritated response, he began to quickly clear his throat before he said a word.

"What the fuck do you want, Mr. Security Man? It better not be too complicated to carry out, or I'm just going to have to flip my 'I don't give a fuck' switch and blast your motherfucking ass right now!"

With a dubious smile, the security officer began to inform Bugsy of what he needed.

"If you're coming up in this motherfucker and snagging a nice, harmless paying customer, maybe you can snag someone else up as well, since you're kidnapping motherfuckers anyway. I have my wife on her way right now to drop me off my lunch. She doesn't have a car because her drunk ass has over six DUIs. So now she drives her mom's beat-up mule that's dying from old age. Everybody laughs at her as she comes down the street ridding that fucking thing. I sometimes can't help it and laugh myself. I have even thrown rocks before, until her forehead shed blood, and then, when I was done, I would hold her tight to me so I could kiss her wounds to make it all better. That dumb bitch would always forgive me no matter what, and I'll always respect that. But now I have no use for her, because I have officially decided that I want to live my life as a careless man whore who don't give a fuck about anybody but myself. So, when she gets here, I was hoping that you could take her with you and make sure she won't ever be seen again as long as I live. I sure would appreciate it, gentlemen, if you could make that happen. Now, do you fellas think you can handle that?"

Bugsy wasn't too excited that he had to put in more work just to get to grandson George. But because that was the only way to shut him up, he had no other choice but to comply.

"Okay, no problem. So, we do this for you and you say nothing. Is that correct?"

"Yes, sir, and I'll even open the door for you on the way out."

Bugsy liked what he was hearing, so he decided to follow through on this small task to make his wish come true.

"Okay, Mr. Security Man, you got a deal, but for right now, the four of us need to go into that theater out back and collect another part of business of our own."

Allowing Bugsy and his mob to go out back and snatch up grandson George was not a big issue for the crazed-minded security officer. He was even grateful enough to get off his hard wooden chair and point out the way. The chair looked as if it had ass-cheek imprints dug into it from many years of sitting on his fat ass and doing absolutely nothing.

"Now, you guys better hurry up and do your thing, and don't take too fucking long, because you still have trash that you have to take out for me."

With all that being said, Bugsy and his mob were finally able to make their way into the back theater to capture grandson George, give him their best ass-kicking, and get all the answers they needed. It wasn't hard to spot his car as they walked past every RV and minivan that every horny douchebag owned and drove into the Stink 'N' the Pink Theater that night. The only reason why people liked driving those types of vehicles into adult drive-in theaters was so they could jack off without being seen. They watched every perverted asshole's love machine vehicle shifting from left to right as they continued to walk towards the Hotchkiss Limousine, where George and his big, fat, pudgy bitch were making out. Bugsy directed the other three to surround the car completely so that George and his bitch would have nowhere to run or hide. With a swift slap of Bugsy old New York Jets Super Bowl ring, hitting the driver-side window, George's attention quickly turned away from his playdate and finally connected eye to eye with Bugsy for the first time in a very long time. The only thing George could do in his response was shake up stiffly until he began to stutter like a little girl, leaving him with only so many words to say.

"Oh no! It's Bugsy!" screamed out George as loud as he could, hoping that someone would come to his rescue. But they were too busy jerking themselves off, like, literately. With all the strength within Bugsy, he quickly drew back his fist and then quickly drove it back into the driver's side window, shattering it so he could yank out grandson George by his big Dumbo ears.

"Hey there, Georgy Girl, are you trying to spice up your life with this big-assed monkey? Maybe you should roll her fat ass up in flour and see if you can find the wet spot first, little buddy."

It was too late. George was finally caught and viciously dragged out of his vehicle to meet the two best friends that Bugsy always had frequently on his mind—Pain and Suffering. It was a brutalizing moment for George, as he was getting hammered by Bugsy's fist intensely, making him bleed from his mouth after knocking out three teeth, just from pounding him repeatedly without a thought of stopping to obtain any medical attention for his worthless needs. In every troubling moment when there is a woman as witness, watching her beloved man getting his ass handed to him by somebody she has never met before, she will always try her best to come to the rescue of her sweetheart lover. And in this case, George's obese woman tried doing just that but failed terribly.

"Please, sir, leave my Georgy alone! We are trying to watch ourselves a romantic movie in peace!"

But Bugsy didn't give a fuck. All she could do was piss and moan as DJ RIP and July teamed up to start beating the shit out of George, because she was too fat to move out of her passenger seat to do anything. Racist Al stood there looking directly into Bugsy's girlfriend's eyes with a boner popping out of his pants as he began to make conversation with her, while the others snatched up George's body to take him back to the Hummer.

"Hey there, my big, beautiful woman! I know a Southern country girl when I see one, and I sure like that dress you're wearing. It reminds me of what my auntie was wearing at our wedding almost ten years back. You think maybe you can take it off for me and play with my dick a bit? Just give it a few twists and jerks for a little personal amusement, please?"

Like the dirty Southern girl that he knew she was, still she played hard to get.

"Well, my name is Branda Chapstick, and the only way you can get me do anything erotic with you is first you have to smell the crack of my ass and tell me out loud that I remind you of your mother so that I can finally tell my whore daughter, Carey, that I'm a much better-performing hooker artist than she will ever be. That dirty bitch is so far off her rocker that the only job she can land is at a fucking yard sale, selling used tampons and pork rinds. Oh, boy, I thought I raised her to be a better professional slut than that, but I guess I was wrong. If only I could find a man in my life to help her become the perfect work of ass, then I would be that man's personal sex slave for the rest of his days on earth."

Racist Al had always dreamed of starting a family, and the way Branda looked at him, hoping desperately that he would agree to step in and play the father figure for her trampy daughter, and maybe even soon be a lunatic husband for herself, he thought that might be possible. She quickly reached down the front of his pants and began to jerk him off slowly, trying to seal the deal before he could even speak a word. She knew that if she could find a way somehow to sweep Racist Al off his feet and make him fall head over heels for her, then the darkness of her days would all be over.

"Hey, baby, I'm not sure If I'm the best role model for any young teenage girl to have around the house. I just might get drunk one day and barge into her room and fuck her living brains out."

And like the Southern crazed whore that she was, she looked

to Racist Al with a smile and growled like a pirate just before she responded, "Don't you worry about that now. I've been prostituting her on the streets since she was ten, and now, she's like an all-American pro! It would be no bother to me at all if you wanted to have a three-way orgasm. It would be a work of art that nobody in the whole world could ever come to do."

Racist Al was touched, and his heart began to soften, as a little teardrop came slowly down his cheek. He would feel very sorrowful and pigheaded if he turned her down and walked away. And so, with no more wasted time, he finally came to a final solution.

"Well, my daddy once told me long ago. He said, 'Son, there will always be a hundred women out there in that world trying to fuck you during your young 'n' reckless days and even throughout your marriage. But one day, you will meet that one and only special half-witted bitch that's willing to be a stay-at-home mom, like a flunky house cat, and put up with your deranged ass while also in taking all-new herpes and crabs that you caught on the streets for her. That woman, son, is called a wife.' And that my beautiful, overweight llama, is what I want to call you for the rest of my cheating-heart days."

Racist Al's loving story was making Branda sweat like a dying pig, and she began playing with her own nipples as Racist Al jumped in the driver seat so he could pull the car out front to meet with the other guys, who already had George and were ready to go.

Every public eye widened up huge upon all their faces as everybody turned to watch Racist Al pulling the car out front. It must have been the loud, squeaky sound of the tires from having too much weight because of Racist Al's obese new bitch being so fucking fat, forcing the bumper to hang low, which was making it scrape across the ground. Nobody in the crowd could stand the awful, annoying sound of the ragged bumper. It was making everybody in the street extremely pissed off and wanting to start a fight, throw rocks, and bitch loudly.

"Hey, man! Kick that big bitch out the fucking car before the tires blow out!" shouted out an old Mexican guy, running a hot dog stand outside the theater. Racist Al didn't like that one bit. The second he heard the discourteous insult that the Mexican hot dog man blabbered from his big mouth, he knew had no other choice but to stop the car, then and there, so he could stick his head out the window to say a few words of his own.

"You better mind your fucking business, Sanchez, before I jump out this car and piss all over your hot dog stand! And when I'm done, I'll just call up immigration to come out here and deport your lazy monkey ass!"

The sounds of roaring thunder and the glare of lighting suddenly came upon the amazing New York City sky, and everybody in sight quickly headed for cover from the nasty rainy weather. Still, that wasn't enough to keep everybody from wanting to be outside. Racist Al and his new hot dog Mexican friend were still in the middle of the street continuing their pointless argument.

"My name is not fucking Sanchez! So stop calling me fucking Sanchez before I drag your girlfriend's fat ass out by her big ham bologna neck and make her deep-throat every one of these delicious fucking hot dogs! And don't talk to me about immigration either, because I was born and raised in America, you little reckless cocksucker!"

Bugsy and the rest of the mob were getting fed up overhearing the idiotic commotion going on in the streets, and Racist Al could hear them from the corner of the sidewalk, trying to persuade him to let it be and to be the better man and walk away. But they all knew that something so simple would not work.

And so, the misfit behavior between the two morons continued on and on.

"Let me ask you something, Sanchez. What the fuck is a Mexican like you doing selling hot dogs anyway? Shouldn't you be out selling tacos, burritos, and stolen car rims?"

"I don't think you're very funny at all, and if you talk shit again, I'm going to kick your fucking monkey ass all over the streets so bad that even your whore mother would feel the tormenting pain and finger herself to her worthless dying sleep. And everybody that's watching within these streets will all stare and laugh to see you cry like the little bitch that you truly are."

The brave asshole that Racist Al was, he slowly got of the car to confront the hot dog man face to face.

"Oh, please don't tell me I'm not funny, because I know I'm funny. Let me tell you a few of my jokes, Sanchez. Maybe you'll like them. What do you call a Mexican with a new car? A felon. Why do Mexican kids walk around school like they own the damn place? Because their dads built it and their moms cleaned it. What do you call a group of stoner Mexicans? Baked beans. Do you want to know why Mexicans like to refry their beans? Because Mexicans can never do anything right the first time. What was the greatest Mexican invention? A solar-powered flashlight. How do you stop a Mexican from robbing your house? Put up a help-wanted sign. And just one more fucking joke, Sanchez: What's the difference between a park bench and a scrubby Mexican like you? That park bench can support a family. What about you, Mr. Smart Mouth Hot Dog Man? Who the fuck supports your family?"

An angry bully look quickly appeared in his squinting eyes as he stupidly continued the pointless conversation between himself and Racist Al.

"Nobody! Supports! My family! But me! You stupid motherfucker! And if I were you, I would get the fuck out of my face right now and just walk away and forget this whole thing ever happened, because if you stay any longer, I'm going to have no choice but to knock you the fuck out and stick my twelve-inch cock up your fat girlfriend's big lard ass! My fucking God, you nasty bastard, that shit is like the back part of an elephant! All meat and no potatoes."

Now Racist Al was very angry, and the only thing on his screwy mind was death. Racist Al couldn't have been more humiliated as he stood out in the middle of the street, getting pissed on by the cold-ass rain and being insulted by an old Mexican guy selling hot dogs on the corner. All the hookers and junkies were still wandering the streets, getting drenched by the rain and looking for their next score. Even they had time to stop and take a moment out of their drug-addicted lives to point and laugh at Racist Al getting clowned on by a strange hot dog guy. So now, with no more funny jokes left to tell, and with all the rage and emotion built inside, he quickly reached into his coat pocket for the Colt six-shooter so he could annihilate him once and for all. Three shoots came firing out quickly from his old beat-up revolver and nailed the poor old Mexican guy once in the throat and twice in the lungs, leaving him with no chance to breathe another lungful of air, and he fell slowly to his knees, then face first on the wet brick. Lots of people were looking out their windows and had witnessed the murder, but it was a shanty part of New York's most-finest rugged neighborhood, and nobody gave a shit. As a matter of fact, all they did was take pictures on their cell phones and thank God it wasn't them. But still, after hearing the gunshots going off from blocks away, the authorities had to show their community that they cared, and so the sounds of sirens suddenly came from the distance, getting closer by the second.

"That's what you fucking get, you piece of shit! Now die next to your hot dog stand and watch me from above robbing your ass of every dollar you made today."

Out of nowhere, Bugsy and the mob pulled up behind Racist Al with the Hummer and shouted at him to get in the truck.

"Come on, man! The fucking cops are coming. We got to get out of here."

And with the best, most respectful manners that Racist Al had, he quickly turned to fat lady Branda and said his last goodbyes.

"I'm so sorry, bitch that I got to do you ugly like this, but I got Sheriff Rosco and the New York police coming this way, and I have no time to bring your fat ass along with me."

The frustration and distress that she felt as soon as she heard those words coming out of Racist Al's mouth made her want to cry a river and vomit all over the inside of the old classic Limousine. She couldn't believe she had wasted even a short amount of time on a loser like Racist Al, hoping that he would be the one to sweep her off her feet and marry her off somewhere far away, in some romantic tropical island and fuck her living brains out. It was just a silly dream that would never happen. But just like any other scene in a sick homeless porn movie, almost every homeless bum crawled out from under their rocks and began trying to cheer up fat lady Branda, hoping that maybe she would give up some sex and let them stay with her at her house so they would never have to be homeless again.

"Hey there, big mama. Forget about that asshole and get with me. I think you have very pretty eyes, and you look like you know how to cook up a good pan of chilly and ride an old man's dick really well. Will you please take me away to your humble home? I haven't had a warm place to live for years!"

Quickly the frustration and distress grew larger, knowing that she was left alone with a bunch of horny homeless dudes who wanted to do nothing but fulfill their own sexual desires and living situations. And so, she was left with nothing else to do but shake her fist in the air and shout and curse as Racist Al slowly walked away to jump into the Hummer.

"You are a lying motherfucker! You said you were going to love me for the rest of my life, and now you're just walking out of my life for good!"

Fat lady Branda was not the only one who was left in total dissatisfaction. The security officer of the theater was watching Bugsy and his mob driving off without keeping their end of the bargain.

"Hey, you motherfuckers! Where and the fuck do you think you're going? You still got a job for me to do, and if you don't do it, I swear to you all, I will kill every single fucking one of you!"

The only feedback the security officer got at that moment was a bunch of assholes sticking their heads out the window and shouting foul and rude comments loudly across the street as they slowly drove away.

"Fuck you, Mr. Security Man! Suck my fucking dick, nigga!" shouted DJ RIP from the rear window. Just when things couldn't get any worse for the outraged security guy, his crazed lunatic wife appeared out of nowhere, riding that beat-up mule that looked like it was running on its last legs and dropping shit bombs all the way to the front door of the theater.

"What the fuck is going on around here? Why are you screaming in the middle of the road and not securing shit at the front gate? Why are there police all over the neighborhood? And who the fuck is this fat bitch stuck in this fancy car right in front of our beautiful theater? I swear to God! I can't leave you here alone to watch over the family theater anymore! You're always fucking shit up when I'm gone. Remember, I'm the boss, and you're my security bitch, and you'll always be my bitch until the day I die! And that day won't be here anytime soon. So until then, you better start doing what your master wife tells you to do, or I'll divorce your ass so quick and take every dime you got! You'll be sleeping on a floor mat at the worst homeless shelter in New York and eating ramen noodles and ketchup out of a trash can faster than you think! So you better get your shit together, or I'm going to throw you out on your ass and jump on your uncle's dick! He always said a rich and greedy Jewish woman like myself should be locked up and sent away to a Holocaust, but maybe a little Hebrew pussy will change his fucked-up Nazi ways."

The security man couldn't believe that he had just gotten burned by some asshole hoodlums, and the only thing he could do was just stand there and listen to the awful bitching voice of his wife, who should have already been dead.

"I'm going to get those sons of a bitches for fucking me over! That bitch should already be dead! That bitch should already be dead!"

After Bugsy and his mob captured George and left the scene in their big black Hummer, July and Racist Al began to stare George down as they held him hostage in the back seat.

"Now listen up, you little fuck! We went all over town looking for you, and we have some questions that need to be answered. So, either you tell us what we need to know, or you can just be another victim."

NINE

Grandson George and the Family Crack House

apturing George had already taken a lot of their valuable time, and to regain what they had lost, they had to make George spit out answers to all their questions as quickly as possible. Doing that would be no problem, but without a caring witness for their beloved hostage, whom they planned on beating the living shit out of, it would be no fun. So, instead of taking him back to their place to torture and kill as per their normal routine, July decided it would be best to meet the family and to get them forcefully involved as well.

"So, where the fuck you live at, kid? We would sure like to meet your family and see the beautiful scenery at your lovely home. Is your mama hot and juicy like a *Hustler* magazine? Or is she just a sloppy housewife that's been passed around a hundred times? What about your siblings! Do you have any slutty albino sisters or any homosexual Chinese brothers?"

George was already frightened, and his idiotic, nerdy ways made him look even stupider as he began to answer their questions.

"Please don't talk bad about my mom, you guys. She really means a lot to me. She's been supporting me my whole life with money, drugs, and sex. It's always a blessing when she brings home top-quality pussy, but if she can't, then she has no shame about putting out herself. And the drugs we get are free! Mama stands over the hot stove almost every night to make a new batch of crack for us to use or sell. And another thing, guys. I'm not Amish, so I don't have any albino sisters, and I'm not from North Korea, so I don't have any homosexual Chinese brothers. I'm an only child! But of course, my parents told me I did have many other half brothers and sisters, throughout the foster-care nation, but they said all those rotten children were just simply fatal mistakes and I should be very lucky to still be a part of this dysfunctional family."

The four of them didn't know quite know what to think about Grandson George, and it didn't take them long to make him show them where he lived. It was a short and joyful ride as they continued their journey to George's house, and as they approached his street, George began to make dumb special requests for his own pleasurable needs.

"Hey, guys, do you think you can pull down this street before we get to my house? All those people down there decorated their Halloween lights so good that it makes the neighborhood light up like a beautiful hydrogen bomb."

Bugsy and the mob were not interested at all in George's fascinating lights, and so they had no choice but to turn down his request.

"Look here, kid! We're not turning down no street to check out some stupid fucking light show! We just want to get you home safe and sound to your lovely parents so we can ask them some questions that you're going to be answering for us. It's really a sit-down talk about your future, kid. Whether you want to continue living in this world or you want to be six feet under. The choice is yours! And when we get to your house, kid, you better start talking quick, because we have been doing enough running around all day, and now there is a lot of crazy shit going down!"

Racist Al had to lay it on him real thick so that George would cut right to the chase as soon as they get him to the house, where they would ask him questions to which they already knew all the answers. But as George continued to sit there still all squashed up in between DJ RIP and Racist Al, he finally decided to ask Bugsy to state his business, i.e., his reason for capturing him.

"Hey, Bugsy, man, you and my Grandpa go back a long time! I don't think he is going to like it very much that you guys fucked up my date and left his car back in that scrubby part of town! He really loved that car, and now he is going to cream me for it—and it was all your guys' fault! So, it's you guys that need to shut the fuck up and start talking! Not me! I don't even know what the fuck is going on! So please, fellas, tell me what the fuck is going on around here, because I don't know a goddamn fucking thing about shit!"

Grandson George may have told them that he didn't know anything about whatever it was they were kidnapping him for, but Bugsy and the mob were not buying it. They felt that he had a lot to do with the murder of his Grandpa Edgar, and because George took that tone with them, DJ RIP made sure he paid for it physically and mentally—for his own good.

"Don't get crazy with us, you little shit! I hate fucking high school kids! And don't tell us that you don't know shit about what the fuck's going on! It was you that was supposed to pick him up at the Senton Hotel that night, and you never did, and that's why your Grandpa's dead—because you had him set up. You sent someone out there to kill his motherfucking ass, nigga! What's a matter, Georgy? Are you starting to remember what the fuck we are talking about now?"

Right away, George's body stiffened up from a quick bitch slap to the face by DJ RIP's backhand. He hadn't known, and he couldn't believe the words coming out of DJ RIP's mouth—that his dearest Grandpa had been killed at the Senton Hotel the other night.

"Oh, my God! My Grandpa is dead? Why in the fuck didn't you just tell me that from the start instead of dragging me out my grandpa's fucking car and ruining my chances of losing my virginity to the most beautiful and fattest woman I have ever met in my life? And then this crazy racist fuck starts sexually touching my girlfriend, and then he starts shooting some fucking hot dog Mexican in the middle of the street! Right where everybody could all see! What in the fuck is a matter with all you guys? Are you all crazy or something? There are other ways to tell someone about a death in the family!"

Bugsy and the mob didn't believe that for one bit. According to them, violence was the only way. After just a few minutes of driving, they were finally at George's house and pulling slowly onto their potholed driveway. All the lights in the house were on, and George could see his mom through the window, sitting peacefully on her wooden rocking chair. After they all got out of the car, Bugsy took over. With great anger, he grabbed George by the back of his neck and began dragging him towards the front door of his lovely home.

The house was small and poorly painted, as if someone had allowed a school bus full of kindergarteners to finger paint rainbows on each side of the house and just leave it there for someone else to clean up. All the stray cats in the yard didn't help the house look any better, either. Bugsy and the mob had to shoo them away continually to keep them from rubbing up against their legs and leaving furball fleas all over their nice paints.

"Come on, Georgy. Let's go see what your mother thinks about you leaving your own grandpa out all night at some lowlife hotel just so you could have him killed. Maybe she will know something about all of this too. What do you think about that, Georgy?"

The only thing left for George to do was kick and scream, hoping Bugsy didn't fill his mom's head with a bunch of bullshit misunderstandings.

"*You* guys got to believe me! I didn't have anything to do with my grandpa's death! I fell asleep! That's why I wasn't there to pick him up."

But Bugsy and the mob still weren't buying it, and the mighty pissed-off mood they were in made it impossible for George to convince them to stop and think a second about the situation.

"Come on, boys! Let's see what kind of skank bitch this motherfucker crawled out from! And she better be young and hot too! I'm not picking any spider webs off her panty hamster," yelled out Bugsy as he began beating the door down with George's scrawny body.

"Hello in there! Is there anybody home? I have your stupid fucking son and some friends of mine out here, and we all want to come in and play with you! So, if you have any brains in that fucking head of yours, you will open now before I get mad-wolf crazy and blow your fucking house down—and then make you blow my dick down!"

Bugsy and the mob didn't have to do any more damage to the front door. George's body had already gone through enough pain from being used as a battering ram. The rattling doorknob began to turn, and when the door opened, everything was more unusual than they had expected.

"Hey there. My name is Andrea Jackoff, but you can call me Mrs. Jackoff! Was that you all pounding on that old door like that? Well, please come in and make yourself welcome, my beautiful little angels. If you have any cat shit on the bottom of your shoes, you better make sure you leave that shit outside! And we don't have any water hose in the backyard either! Now, I hope you boys like hot cocoa and caramel apples with nuts! Because we have a lot of it."

Bugsy and the mob were shocked that George's mom. She seemed overjoyed about everything, especially after she had seen the beating they put on George.

"Oh, hello, Georgy, my sweetest son. Did you tell these nice gentlemen thank you for bringing you home? Looks like you must have been talking their ears off the whole drive here! That's probably why they waked you. I used to do it to him too, except I used a tortilla roller on his ass to crack that noggin. So, how do you handsome men know a strange, creepy little boy like my son, George?"

Bugsy was so pleased that Mrs. Jackoff had given them such a great greeting, and the caramel apples with nuts were going down smoothly with his cup of hot cocoa. Bugsy didn't want to come off too strong when telling Mrs. Jackoff that her father had been killed the other night, and because she had treated them so well, he decided to break the awful news to her in his most respectful manner possible.

"I need to tell you something, Mrs. Jackoff. I know that me and you don't know each other at all or whatsoever, but I'm here to tell you that I was very close to your father, Edgar. We have been doing business together now for over ten years with our very own secret family organization. Your daddy never told you about it because he said you were a lying skanky whore, just like your mother, and you could never be trusted. But anyway, he always told me so much about you and how beautiful you always are. Just hearing the way your daddy would always describe you to me every time he spied on you in the shower was very pleasant and always brought cum to my pants. Oh, Andrea, I wish I was here to tell you some good news, but unfortunately, I'm not. I think you should sit down for this, because I have some devastating news to inform you about your dear old father and our loving boss. He was fucking murdered last night! At a rundown hotel. Only George knows what happened, and he's not telling us fucking shit!"

Mrs. Jackoff couldn't believe her ears. Hearing the news about her father's murdering death brought tears to her eyes and chills all over her body. Bugsy made sure to comfort her as quickly as he could before she found another shoulder to cry on. It was one of his methods that he would use to get a girl to sleep with him. He hoped that maybe if he acted nice enough, showing he had true emotions and really cared about a bitch's feelings, maybe she would be nice enough to lay him.

"Easy now, Mrs. Jackoff. I myself also know how it feels like to lose a loved one, except my wife wasn't murdered by somebody else. I did that shit myself, and not a day goes that I don't wish I could do it again. But anyway, Mrs. Jackoff, we all must face reality. We must live with the fact that your father, our boss, is dead. The only thing we can do about it right now is beat the living shit out of your son, George, for some goddamn answers! He was one of the last ones to see your father before he was murdered the other night, and he's not saying shit! He was supposed to pick up Edgar that night at the hotel, but he never did. He said he fell asleep, but I say he is full of fucking shit and he had his own grandpa set up and killed! We all feel that he just might know something that we don't know, Mrs. Jackoff, and we're going to need your help to make him cooperate with us."

The evil-bitch face that Mrs. Jackoff made as she turned quickly to look at George scared Bugsy and the mob half to death. There was no telling how mad she really was, and there was nobody to hold her down either as she jumped out of her seat to yank George by his ear.

"You left your grandpa at a fucking scrubby hotel in the middle of the night and you forgot to pick him up? George Annabella Jackoff, that doesn't sound like something you would normally do! Why in the fuck were you two at that hotel in the first place? And you better tell me the truth, or I'll take away all your jerkoff magazines for a month this time."

George's eyes widened quickly when he heard his mother make that threat about his jerkoff magazines. He knew he had to speak up and tell them everything he knew, or he would have to live with his own devastating personal consequences.

"Okay, bitch! Goddamn! I'll tell you guys everything. I dropped grandpa off at the Senton Hotel because he wanted to meet up with some hooker that was going to suck his dick off for his sixty-ninth birthday. And yes, he did tell me to pick him up back at the hotel within two hours, but I never made it because I fell asleep. I'm very, very, sorry! It was another one of my special magazines again, Mom! I couldn't help myself! It was called *The Dirty, Horny Secrets of Theodore Roosevelt.* I whacked off really good, and I enjoyed every minute of it! It felt so good that I accidentally fell asleep. About four hours later, after I finally woke up and realized that I had overslept and forgot to pick up Grandpa, I figured only two things. One: he probably hit somebody else up for a ride home. Or two: he also was feeling so good that he fell asleep as well. How in the fuck was I supposed to know this was going to happen? Don't try to blame this shit on me!"

Right away, without even thinking twice about it, Mrs. Jackoff knew exactly how to calm the situation down in her own special way.

"Okay, everybody, chill … the … fuck … out and follow me to the kitchen! I have the most wonderful surprise that's just going to lighten up our minds so that we can all be at peace with each other and not at war!"

Everybody looked to each other and quickly gathered around Mrs. Jackoff to slowly follow behind her into her kitchen.

"Welcome to our kitchen, where our family produces some of the finest crack rock that you ever used in your whole life. This base is called the Crazy Cougar. I smoked so much of this shit that one time I invited in the newspaper boy in for a sex-and-wine party. His parents and teachers didn't like that too much, and I had to take my family and move far away from our community. It was such a terrible time for George in that awful year. Every kid at school would come up to him and ask for my number, wondering if they could plow me. Anyway, I blabber on too much. How about all of us smoke on this beautiful golden nugget until we hear the sweet crackling sounds. We all had a hard day, gentleman, and I think that we all owe it to ourselves to enjoy this wild ride, because if we don't, some other scrounged-up mooching bum will."

Bugsy couldn't believe everything George had said about his mom making loads of crack over the oven was actually true. So now, with Mrs. Jackoff's purple glass crack pipe loaded up with the finest golden nuggets, she looked to Bugsy and handed it to him with both hands flat out, as if she were granting him the sword of honor. A light shined over Bugsy at that moment as he gently grabbed the loaded crack pipe from the palms of her hands. He realized there really were great people who looked out for each other, and with a quick slap to the back of Mrs. Jackoff's ass, he looked at her with a smile and began to smoke up their best-produced crack, which they called the Crazy Cougar.

"Oh …! Fuck yeah! It's like having sex without a condom for the first time! You fuckers got to try this shit! It's going to blow you away."

Quickly the others gathered around Bugsy to help him smoke Mrs. Jackoff's Crazy Cougar crack. After they had all taken a few hits apiece, their minds began to feel more loving and raunchier, and before they knew it, they were then gathered around Mrs. Jackoff to rub their hands up her short red skirt.

"Please, guys, not around George I wouldn't want the little bastard running off and telling his father! Maybe we should continue to clear up some more of my father's business first. George, honey! Remember how you said Grandpa was at the hotel to meet up with some hooker? Well, who exactly was this hooker that he was meeting up with?"

George paused as soon as he heard his mom ask the name of the hooker that his grandpa had met up with that night.

"Oh, I don't know. Just another street rat trying to make a living, I guess."

Mrs. Jackoff always knew when her son was lying, and with another yank by the ear, she got him to spill his guts all over again. It didn't take long.

"Look here, you little fucking shit! You have a dead grandpa that was brutally killed, and you're going to tell me who this whore is right goddamn now!"

The pulling of the ears was becoming much too painful for George. He had no choice but to tell his cracked-out mother the other half of the story.

"All right, you fucking crack whore! The bitch that Grandpa was meeting up with is a very sweet and beautiful lady that goes by the name Scarlet! But most people know her as Koko. She was the last one who could have been with Grandpa the other night at the hotel. None of you guys better lay a fucking hand on her! She would never kill Grandpa. They have been client and customer for a long time now, and she was evening kind enough to let me watch and jerk off a few times. It was all so wonderful, watching Grandpa driving his dick in a sexy hooker's pussy while I stood behind the bushes, cheering him on and on! It was better than banging horses at the Kentucky Derby!"

George's mother wasn't too pleased about everything that he

was getting himself into, and she couldn't believe that her father had been cheating on her mom for several years now. Just knowing that her father had always been a cheating bastard made her so angry that she demanded George tell her where she could find the trampy little hooker who everybody knew as Scarlet.

"Georgy, you reckless little bitch! You better tell your mother right now where to find that skanky female dog before I give you more lickins upside your head!"

Of course, George caved in like a little bitch and told his crack whore mother everything that he knew about his dream girl, Scarlet.

"Me and Grandpa found her on the Live Links hotline several years back, and she's been doing personal odd business with us ever since. I even have her personal number that she gave me, but Grandpa don't know about that, but I guess he knows now! Haha … Oh shit! I hope he don't return from the dead and kill me for that one. He wouldn't be too proud of me, but I don't give a rat's shit!"

Without saying a word, Mrs. Jackoff bitch-slapped George across his face and snatched the number from his hands.

"Well, looks like no loose juicy pussy for you, my son, and let that be a lesson to you! I will give this number to this nice gentleman and his mob and let them be on their way. You have to excuse me for no longer wanting to know your names, but anybody tied up in the mob? I'd just rather not know too much about anything or anyone, especially out here in the city of New York."

George's broken heart was now filled with blistering rage after watching his own mother hand over the phone number of his wet fantasy dream girl to Bugsy and his mob. He couldn't believe that his own mother would betray him like that. The fact she might have murdered his grandpa no longer mattered to him at all. The only thing running through his mind at that moment was pure vengeance against everyone and everything in the house. So now, with all his angry emotions, he quickly pushed his mother into the cooking stove, knocking over all the crack pots to the floor and even causing his mother's hair to catch on fire from the high flames rising from the surface of the stove. The place was beginning to smell like burned hair and no longer like plastic and chemicals, and Bugsy and the mob wanted nothing to do with it. So, out of shock and fear, Bugsy and the mob grabbed a fistful of little crack baggies from the kitchen table and bailed out as soon as they could without a thought of saving Mrs. Jackoff from her crazed lunatic son, George. So now, with another kitchen of another house going up in flames for the second time in just one night, all Bugsy could do was give his last fair-well goodbye.

"Sorry, Mrs. Jackoff, but this here is a family problem, and we don't want nothing to do with it. So, if you don't mind, we going to get out of your fiery hair right now and leave you two alone. Maybe you two should watch the *Dr. Phil Show* together and check into a nuthouse! That's what my psychologist told me once. I know, Mrs. Jackoff, that you hate to see me go and love to watch me leave, but this is the end of the road for you—and us. I hope you have a nice journey into your own personal and unnatural afterlife! Thank you and good riddance!"

Like every crackhead bitch, she had to get the last word.

"You motherfuckers! How dare you all, leave me to burn to death with this whacked-out fucking son of mine! I'll come back from the dead and kill all of you for letting me die so painfully and horribly, and you will never enjoy the moments of being alive ever again!"

Listening to Mrs. Jackoff slowly dying did not bother them. They had finally got what they came for, and once again, they all walked away slowly from another burning house of victims and shame.

Edgar's Funeral

5 days later

After they had all left another smoky house burning in flames, Bugsy thought it would be best to postpone the strike on Scarlet for a while so they could plan everything out and pay their respects to their boss, Edgar. It has been five days now since they had killed anyone or even eaten any human flesh, and the last chances they'd had to bring home any delicious human meat they'd let burn to deaths in their own homes.

Later that day, in the early afternoon, Bugsy finally got the call from Mr. Corpse Bandit, the funeral home director at Dead Cheap Family Funeral Home Services.

"Hey, Bugsy! This is Mr. Corpse Bandit down at the human parts funeral sale! Oh, shit, you must excuse me! I didn't mean to say all that! What I meant to say was ... down at our lovely funeral home, your friend Edgar, sir, is prepared and ready for our funeral home services. We will be ready for all his friends and family to join us tomorrow morning at 9:00 a.m. for the wake. Don't worry about the burial. We'll be driving his body out to Dead Thug Cemetery in our very own special 1918 Dain Tractor—the very first old piece of shit tractor that John Deer produced way back in the good old beat-your-wife days!"

Bugsy was so pleased to finally hear that everything was ready and that he could make phone calls to almost everyone in Edgar's personal directory book. Even though it was very late notice, Bugsy still tried to gather as many friends and family members as he could.

"Thank you so much, Mr. Corpse Bandit! You have no idea how bad I want to get this over with, and you have no idea how hard this has been for all of us. We will give our friend Edgar the best damn funeral any deadbeat fuck has ever had!"

Bugsy was overjoyed as he hung up the phone with Mr. Corpse Bandit. He could not wait to tell the others.

"Good news gentlemen. Edgar's funeral is tomorrow at 9:00 a.m.! So make sure to wear something respectful! And don't come empty handed either! Bring a gift card or some fucking flowers! Mr. Edgar would really like something like that."

The rest of the mob was overjoyed as well and could not wait for the next day to come. But now they had another problem—finding something respectful to wear, because everything they were wearing was stained with blood and smelled like death, crack, and whores. The only guy in the mob with any idea of what they all should wear for tomorrow's funeral was DJ RIP, because none of the other guys had a fucking clue.

"Hey, everybody, I can tell just by looking at all your faces that none of you motherfuckers have a clue what to wear! But I sure do, and if any of you all want in on it, then we need to leave now, because the best place to shop for times like this will close in the next couple of hours. And I'm a picky shopper. That means I don't like to be rushed! So, come on if you like, and I'm fucking driving to Bugsy's! Don't be all stingy with the truck! You think I like people seeing a black man sitting in the back all the fucking time?"

After hearing DJ RIP's last-call announcement about the dress-code situation, they all quickly gathered their things and headed out the front door. Before any of the others could say anything, Bugsy yelled, "Shotgun" and hopped in the front set as the rest followed behind.

"All right, you all! We out this motherfucker! And if any of you punk-ass bitches forgot to use the bathroom, then you better point your dicks out the window and start to piss, because I'm not pulling over for shit! The sooner we can get to this place, the sooner we can leave and get home so I can smoke my weed and watch my *I Love Lucy* show. I really wish they didn't close so damn early, but the owner always says he's got another side job going on, and he has nobody else to run the store while he's away."

It wasn't a long drive to the clothing store that DJ RIP referred them to. As soon as they all pulled up out front, they couldn't wait to get out, seeing all the great and amusing stuff they had on display in the windows and all the weird things sitting outside as well. The store was meant for having all kinds of crazy shit, and that's why the owners called their unwanted business the Creep Master Shopping Store. It was the only unusual store like that in town, and it attracted many tourists from all over the nation.

"All right, my niggas. This is it! The Creep Master Shopping Store. Now don't spend too much time checking out stupid shit! Remember, we still have to find something to wear for Edgar's funeral, and it will close less than a couple of hours, so you all better make it fast and sweet, because I don't feel like staying all fucking day in this creepy fucking place!"

The store wasn't all that big, but it wasn't small either, and it was very hard to avoid some of the odd things that they had for sale, like the Finger Pussy Monkey Paw and a jar of ashes that they claimed it belongs to the dead dog Toto from *The Wizard of Oz* movie. There was even a bright pink twenty-inch dildo that was hanging off a ceiling fan. Everybody in the store said it belonged to a lady named Mango Truman—the very first lady in the state of New York to have ever sat on a twenty-inch object and survived to enjoy it. It was like a work of art in the eyes of so many perverted people, who were browsing around the store at that time and day.

After about forty-five minutes of looking at and trying on suits in their deep-freezer fitting rooms, they finally found what they were looking for. Dj RIP walked out of the Creep Master Shopping Store with a smile on his face, knowing that he wouldn't be missing one second of his favorite *I Love Lucy* show.

"Hell, yeah, my niggas! We got ourselves some fucking boom-ass clothes, huh? And for so fucking cheap, too! I think we owe it to ourselves to go home and roll a big fat blunt of this new shit that I call *smoke acid*! It has a lot of cactus medicines and other nutritious shit! Don't worry, though. The journey won't last that long."

The others looked at each other as if they probably shouldn't try this new experience, but even more so, they all agreed that DJ RIP was full of shit.

As soon as they got back to the house, everybody realized how early in the day it still was, and they didn't want to waste any time talking about memories of Edgar and being in mourning and what not. Throughout the whole car ride home, they listened to DJ RIP talk a big story about his weed being so great, and now they couldn't wait to get started on rolling that blunt.

"Hey, Mr. DJ RIP, let's get started on that sweet little blunt that you were talking about! We all got our suits, and I'll even order a pizza! Your television show starts in a couple of hours, and I think we should all be set throughout the rest of the day without anything else to worry about, so let's get on that shit now!" shouted Bugsy with joy. But DJ RIP didn't want to get started quite yet, and the holdup was just pissing everybody off.

"Not yet, man! I need to get settled first! First, I need to take a huge shit! And then jerk it! And then nap! For like two hours—until my show comes on! After that, then we can smoke. I love watching the *I Love Lucy* show when I'm fucking high! So, does that sound like a plan or what?"

The others had no choice but to wait. Out of anger and impatience, they all quickly reached into the ice freezer and grabbed the five frozen packs of maple link sausages and began throwing them directly at DJ RIP's head for building up their spirts and then making them wait.

"Fuck you, DJ RIP! I wanted to do this shit right now! But you got to act like a little bitch about it, don't you? I'll tell you right now, if you don't have your shit together by the time your show starts, then we are all kicking your ass and taking your blunt! And don't you be thinking that we're going to wait to order the pizza, because we are all hungry, and we're going to order that shit right now! And you can have whatever the fuck is left of the pizza after we are all done fucking it with our dicks, and then we will leave it nice and cold for you in the fridge! Now, how does that plan sound, motherfucker?" shouted Bugsy.

DJ RIP sure didn't like the way Bugsy and the others were talking about him, and because of that, he felt he had to set an example for them.

"All right, motherfuckers! You all want to play that fucking game with me? Now I'm going to use the only bathroom that we got in this house for the whole two hours that I'm making you wait for, and don't even try knocking on the door to rush me out, because I'm not going anywhere! You all are going to have to go out back and use old rolled-up newspaper for toilet tissue! Haha. How do all you motherfuckers like me now?"

The others didn't like that idea at all, and so they quickly put their heads together to come up with a well-laid plan for DJ RIP. July had the perfect idea for dealing with DJ RIP's asshole behavior.

"Okay, everybody, come close and listen up, because I don't want this motherfucker to overhear a single word that we're talking about. I have one Judas's belt outback in the tool shed that stretches out about six feet long, and I also got some bloom flower ground spinners! I say we smoke him out! If that motherfucker wants to blow up our bathroom in such bad taste and disrespect, then he needs to earn each and every one of those valuable seconds that he sits on that toilet set, enjoying his sweet and healthy shit! Now, are you all with me or not?"

Unfortunately, the first one to respond was Racist Al, because the rest of them were beginning to have second thoughts upon starting shit with DJ RIP. They knew he wouldn't go down without a fight, and if they fucked with him, they would most defiantly have to expect retaliation—and that is something they simply didn't want. It would be getting caught in the middle of a war zone—just like July would want it to be.

"Hell, yeah, man! I'm with you! Whatever you need to make this happen, I'll be at your services. Besides that, boy needs a real good lesson taught to him!"

Just hearing those words out of Racist Al's mouth brought a smile to July's face, as he could now declare his war of independence. Calling the rest of the mob to follow him into the back where the toolshed stood, he quickly pulled both shed doors out, as far as they could go, and told them to gather all the fireworks out of the Christmas box and follow him right back inside the house.

"Okay, this is what we are going to do. I'm going to take these six feet Judas's belts right here, and I'm going to shove them right under the bathroom door and light those motherfuckers up! The rest of you guys, I'll need you to light up as many as these ground spinners as you can in the middle of the hallway, so that when he comes running out of this bathroom, screaming like a little bitch, he will have nowhere to run or hide, and then that's when we ambush him! And when I say ambush, I mean we all jump in and beat the living shit out of him! Now, do you all think you can handle this small task?"

They already had everything all ready to go. There was no way they could back out now, because if anybody did, he would be looked at like he was the biggest pussy in the world, and none of them wanted that kind of reputation for themselves, especially coming from a great military veteran like July.

"No problem, July. Start pushing those belts under the door, and start lighting up that shit now. Me and Bugsy will get started on these ground spinners," whispered Racist Al. So now the only the thing left to do so set a fiery grand finale in the bathroom where DJ RIP was sitting peacefully, taking a nice healthy shit, was just simply to take a lighter to the end of the fuse, and so, with great pride and honor, July quickly put the fire to the fuse with a devilish smile on his face, then calmly waited for the first set of fireworks to go off.

"What the fuck, man! Who the fuck is doing that shit? I think

I'm getting blisters on the back of my ass!" yelled DJ RIP. For a few brief seconds, July almost felt sorry for him, but he just reminded himself about the two-hour wait that DJ RIP was trying to force upon them. So, the next moment, he ordered Bugsy and Racist Al to start lighting up the bloom flower ground spinners so that when DJ RIP walked out the bathroom door, they would all be ready for him, and it would make it easier to kick his ass without him really expecting it. And so, now again, with the second set of fireworks going off, the entire house was now covered in smoke from everything they lit off outside the bathroom door. Green, red, purple, and blue were all sparkling brightly and spinning round and round on the hallway floor, making the three of them jump for joy like a bunch of kids. After the last of the fireworks went out, they stood silently together by the bathroom door, waiting desperately for it to swing open so they could all begin the process of kicking DJ RIP's ass. He wouldn't come out right away, and after a few minutes of waiting for him to come out, Racist Al lost his patience and began to kick the bottom of the door as hard as he could with his steel-toed boots.

"I don't know which one of you motherfuckers did all this crazy shit! And I don't know which one of you motherfuckers is kicking the fucking door! But when I get done wiping my burned and blistered ass, I'm going to beat the living fuck out of all of you for doing this shit to me!"

It was now almost certain that they had no other choice but to jump in all at once and get the very best beating out of him, because if they tried fighting DJ RIP one on one at that moment, in his state of mind, then it would be all over for them, and they all knew it. So, to make themselves feel a little more comfortable, they quickly looked around to find something more suitable to wear around their knuckles. The smoke throughout the house was making it hard for them to see, and before they knew it, they all began to hear the sounds of a doorknob unlocking. And as they hurried back over to the bathroom to wait for DJ RIP to slowly walk out, they could not see the toilet seat in his hands from all the smoke. The first one out of the three to take one for the team was none other than Racist Al himself.

"Goddamn, motherfucker! What the fuck did you hit me with? Well, don't just stand there, you two! Kick DJ RIP's fucking teeth in!"

And so now, with one man down and the other two still standing tall before DJ RIP, who was looking directly at them, holding the toilet seat tightly in his hands, the other two had no doubt whatsoever. Without any hesitation, Bugsy and July both came at DJ RIP with everything they had, trying their best to out-battle him, just like they said they would.

The fight was brutal. DJ RIP was swinging away rapidly with the hard toilet seat as Bugsy and July both hung in there like tag-team wrestlers. Blood began to immediately squirt out of Bugsy's and July's head from the beating with the toilet seat, and as they tried their hardest to work together, they wound up taking him to the ground by rushing him as quickly as they could, causing his legs to wobble until he finally dropped to the floor, making the toilet seat slip out of his hands.

"All right, Bugsy! We got this motherfucker to the ground! Now keep him there, and don't let him back up! I'm going to teabag his fucking face!"

As Racist Al milked his injuries, leaving the others to fight the battle against DJ RIP, he quickly looked around for something to bash in his head with. The only thing he saw laying on the ground was the same toilet seat that he got whacked with. Without any second thought, he reached down slowly to pick it up.

"Oh, look what we got here! Now it's your turn, DJ RIP, to get hit with the toilet seat! Now, just hold still, you little fuck rag! And don't scream! This will only take a second."

But DJ RIP was too smart, and he managed to get out of the grip that Bugsy had him in. When Racist Al took a fast swing, he accidentally hit Bugsy across the face, knocking him to the ground.

"You motherfuckers can't take me on! I'm the craziest nigga in New York City, and I'll be goddamned if three white crackers could kick my ass!"

The little task that July had well planned out was no longer so little, and they realized that they had bitten off more than they could chew. But in almost every great battle, there is a hero that comes out of nowhere to save the day, and in this situation, July was that lucky person. He decided that he was going to finish what he'd started. And so, he grabbed the fire extinguisher that he saw hanging on the empty fish tank and broke off the safety pin. Now, looking at DJ RIP with his back facing towards him, he then squeezed the operating lever to hose him down, unleashing everything that was left inside the extinguisher until he dropped to his knees, shaking.

Suddenly the tables had turned. At that moment, it almost looked as if DJ RIP's life was over, as Racist Al stood over him with the bright red fire extinguisher, getting ready to bash his head in with it. But out of good grief, the others wouldn't allow it. They managed to stop Racist Al before he could get off that last swing, probably feeling there was no longer any point to the fight and because they knew DJ RIP had the magic weed that so desperately wanted to try. So now, with the fight finally under control, Bugsy quickly got himself mentally and physically situated back to his normal self so he could preach a few things.

"First of all, I just want to say, out of great respect, that it was very close, and a fair fight. I feel that I got some great education here, and I think that calls for a happy joint celebration! Come on, DJ RIP, let bygones be bygones and forget this ever happened! What do you say? Are we amigos again or what?"

DJ RIP already knew that they were just kissing ass so they could smoke his finest smoke acid weed, but that didn't matter, because it would be a lot less painful than taking hits from a metal fire extinguisher.

"Man, what in the fuck has gotten into all you motherfuckers? I can't take a shit in peace for one second because some stupid motherfuckers want to set off fireworks in the bathroom! I won't be able to sit down nice and comfortable for like a fucking month, man, because of you guys and your fucking kid games! And now you all want me to share my weed with you! Yeah, okay! Let's smoke some fucking weed! And you guys better be able to keep up with me, because I'm the motherfucking weed master out here in New York

City, and nobody can out-smoke me, because I'm the Beast of the East! Everybody knows that."

So now, with everything seemingly back to somewhat normal, DJ RIP finally decided to pull out his killer weed that he had been talking so highly about. The other three gazed at the joint as DJ RIP slowly put it to his lips and prepared for liftoff. Watching the fire off his Hanna Montana lighter made all their mouths drool like cocker spaniels, and when DJ RIP reached out to pass the joint, it almost became another royal rumble, watching them fight over who got to smoke next.

"All right, bitches! Shut the fuck up! I'll decide who gets to smoke this next, and because I'm a man who always plays fair, we will flip for it with this shiny brown penny that I found inside the crap bowl of a Porta Potty at the Woodstock '99 festival. It's my favorite penny! It brings me good luck but smells like shit to everybody else. And the way we flip for this, gentleman, is easy! I'm going to flip this coin here up in the air, and the first person to grab it after it hits the ground will get to smoke this badass motherfucker next! So, are all you guys ready? I'll count down from three, okay! And three, two, one, go ...!"

Watching and absorbing the shiny, brown penny floating in the air and debating where it will land made the coin toss game a little more intense, and as they all began to shove each other out the way, trying their best to scramble for the coin, it was soon recovered by July, who walked back over to DJ RIP with the winning coin to exchange for the next puffs of the smoke acid joint.

"Here, motherfucker! Take this shit-smelling penny and pass me that joint!" shouted July. And when he put the joint to his lips and took a few hits, it was already over. The DMT that DJ RIP had planted in his well-made joint was beginning to take a turn on himself and July. The other two couldn't wait to smoke next. The trip was very outer space for all of them. Everything that they looked at was all shined up, with heavy brightness, and every time they took a step closer to something or someone, it was as if the earth had come to life and dragged them farther and farther away. Their bodies could no longer move, and they just collapsed on the ground like sacks of potatoes.

DMT is usually more effective when lying on your back and looking up at the sky. At first, it feels like you have no control over your own body, but the sooner you keep reminding yourself that you're on DMT, the better off you're going to be. It was just too bad that the three of them were all new to the experience, and the more they smoked, the farther they fell into a world of weirdness and unexplained visitors from God-knows-where. They were about to flip into freak-out mode and possibly do some crazy-ass shit, but DJ RIP knew how to bring the trip down a bit. Hidden in his secret place where he kept most of his personal belongings, he pulled out a bottle of Early Times Kentucky Whisky and made them all drink as much as they could to bring them back to earth and restore their stable thinking.

Well, maybe not exactly *stable* thinking. But at least they knew what planet they were on, and they wouldn't have to worry about the 1958 Central Railroad train running through their fucking living room or even hearing voices of stubborn old ladies hurdling cows in the backyard. Their short journey was taking them for a spin, and all the liquor that DJ RIP had told them to drink wasn't doing much help at all. Each of them was suddenly beginning to see his own personal visions, and there was no telling what they would do next.

Bugsy's vision was some kind of a crazed fellowship get-together, where some of the all-time most dangerous dictators and mobsters, like Joseph Stalin, Benito Mussolini, Hideki Tojo, Al Capone, Lucky Luciano, John Gotti, Pablo Escobar, and Tony 'Big tuna' Accardo, all came in to visit Bugsy and talked to him about how a good job he was doing and even dropping him pointers on how to kill more people. It was a very proud and honorable moment for Bugsy, and he didn't want the trip ever to end.

Racist Al had another wild trip. His vision was also very weird and intense, watching burning crosses appearing in front of his eyes and marching around him in circles, singing the Horst Wessel tune that represented the German Nazi anthem. Suddenly he was filled with joy, and he began dancing and shouting to the moon, calling out all the dead Jews from the Holocaust to rise from their unmarked graves so that he could kill them all over again.

July's vision was altogether different. Seeing everybody that he had killed as a soldier during his first tour in Afghanistan put a smile on his face—in addition to seeing his own mother getting fucked in her ass by a drunken maniac dressed in a Santa Claus suit, shouting at her, "You have been a very slutty whore for Christmas! You have been a very crazy bitch for fucking Christmas!"

And his mother would do nothing but take it in the ass as she stared at her son July, yelling, "What the fuck are you looking at, junior? I'm doing this to put food on the fucking table! So you better start being more appreciative and stay out of trouble! Oh, my Lord, the things a mother must do to support her own children these days! What the fuck is this goddamn world coming to?"

The only thing July did was stand there with a smile and ask his mother if it was okay to watch.

"Don't mind me, Mother. If it's all right with you, I would like to just sit here and watch. I always enjoyed watching you and Daddy fucking. I would be hidden in the closet, and you wouldn't even know, and I would just be whacking off and off repeatedly. I would say at least five times a week."

DJ RIP's vision wasn't as crazy as the others, but it had its moments, and he enjoyed every bit of it. His ears were shaped like that of an elf, he had the body of a black grizzly bear, and he could hear turntables scratching and bass pumping and vibrating out throughout the whole house. It was like a flashback to the 80s party. Everybody was breakdancing and snorting cocaine. Everything looked fantastic, but there was only one main thing that caught his eye, and that was a very beautiful lady, standing all alone far in the back of the corner of the room. Her name was Nichole, and she was half Japanese prostitute and half killer wolf. She came from a tribe called the Moon Blood Maniacs, and everybody knew her as Nichole the Hoe because of her bitchy attitude. So now, being so horny and blood thirsty, she called out to him to drive his attention to her.

"Yo! DJ RIP! Bring your black ass over here and bum rush the show on me, big boy! And maybe I'll play with your big daddy dick until it pukes all over my mouth! What do you say, baby? Do you want to come party with me?"

The trip was going beautifully for him. It was just too bad that it had to end so quickly. The booze that they were drinking so much of finally kicked in, and they were now just a fistful of drunken idiots still slowly coming off their trip, all very angry that it ended so quickly. But Bugsy put them back in their place with another of his wonder-full-of-shit speeches.

"Don't worry, gentlemen. We had a good trip, and we can continue our party! Nobody says we must stop! So, let's keep drinking all the way, until the funeral is said and done. The sooner it's all over, the sooner we can track down Scarlet."

None of them ever caved in from their cheap hard liquor. They stayed drunk all the way up to the time the funeral started.

ours and hours went by. Nine o'clock was only a half hour away, and the great and mighty drunken Bugsy ordered the others to grab all their belonging and pile into the truck as quickly as they could.

"Hey! Attention, everybody! We need to be at the funeral in about a half hour! So, grab your cheap dime monkey suits and get in the fucking truck! You can change on the way there!"

After hearing that, the others showed no sign of wasting any more valuable time. They grabbed everything they needed and headed out the door to hurry into the truck. They also didn't show any sign of wasting any liquor, because that was one of the main items each of them brought with him. They all wanted to show respect for Edgar's death and give him one last drink before they put him into the ground of his own grave.

With Bugsy behind the wheel, as usual, they skated off into the foggy morning, and with the high beams not working on the Hummer, Bugsy's drunk ass had a hard time seeing, but he wasn't that far away, because his navigator led right to the funeral home. When they finally found it, they made one hell of an entrance. Mr. corpse Bandit didn't like it one bit. Arriving to the place was one thing, but crashing the Hummer into the front entrance door just because you felt that you deserved front-row parking was another thing. That was exactly what they did, and when they all slowly climbed out of the Hummer, they acted like nothing ever happened, and they went on smelling and failing at mourning in their own characteristic ways, as they walked into the doors of the Dead Cheap Funeral Home's parlor.

Mr. Corpse Bandit reacted quickly to the fatal crash that had just destroyed his entire beautiful front door entrance. It was the only thing that made the funeral home stand out, so it didn't look so ragged and cheap, and now Mr. Corpse Bandit was very angry with Bugsy and the mob.

"You stupid fucking sons of bitches! What in the fucking God's hell have all you fucking ass clowns done to my new custom-made door? I just got this put in last week! You stupid dumb fucks! Oh! this is going to be added to your death bill, and I'm going to make sure that none of your deadbeat loved ones ever get treated at my family's overrated funeral home ever again!"

But Bugsy and the mob didn't care. They just rudely bowled past him and told Mr. Corpse Bandit to mind his own business in their own drunken way.

"Look here, buddy! I don't give a rat's fuck about your scrubby family's funeral home! So you better just mind your goddamn business, boy, before I wring you by your neck and drag you away to a dark closet and molest you like a fucking runaway drag queen! Don't worry, though. I'll make sure your sexy little ass doesn't feel a solitary thing! Your name will be Laura Ingalls, and I'll dress you up as my farm girl! You will be climbing underneath a pregnant cow and milking me a fucking gallon of milk every day. And when you're done milking my cow, I'll make your tight little ass skip right over to me and make you pour me a glass. You will be singing a pretty little song too! Something queer that I know you like. "Dancing

Queen" by ABBA. Yeah! I know you like that one, woman! You're going to make a wonderful wife for a very wonderful man one day! And I hope, my darling, you can find it in your heart to make that wonderful man be me! I would treat you very nice, I promise! Your nightmares shall never be forgotten, my love!"

Mr. Corpse Bandit no longer had any respect whatsoever for Bugsy at that moment, and he acknowledged that fact right away. He even whistled over to the rest of his staff to come out and stand by his side, just so he could even out the odds a little bit, in case Bugsy and his mob wanted to get physical.

"Now you listen to me, Bugsy! What you said out of your mouth, boy, was pure fucking death words. Me and my new organized mob, who now go by the name of Satan's Grave-Robbing Pirates, are going to make you all join the rest of those dead stupid fucks that are all rotting six feet under! We will let you faggots pay your respects to your old pal Edgar! And when you leave, you better take his dead wrinkled ass with you, because if you leave him here, we going to stuff his ass like a roadkill possum and make him our little sex puppet! We'll call him Old Man Pinocchio! He can tell us lies anytime he wants, because our assholes will love the feeling of his big, long nose going in and out of our ass! It will always be memorable."

ELEVEN

A New War Begins

Bugsy and the mob didn't want to stay a minute longer, and so they did what Mr. Corpse told them to do. They all walked quickly to the coffin, grabbed Mr. Edgar's body out, and held him up high in the air, then slowly walked him out through the caved-in the wall that they had crashed into. The short friendship that Bugsy and Mr. Corpse Bandit had was now out the window, and you could fairly say that the dispute between both sides was now in session. Somehow, and so quickly, the word was out all over the streets of New York, and every bum and foster kid would soon be passing out the handmade newspapers of their own photos and journalism. The main attraction that caught the eye of the mob was the very front of the paper, which read in big words:

It's Another Street Turf War between the One and Only Cannibal Mafia and the Newest Sick-Minded Mothers Fuckers: Satan's Grave-Robbing Pirates.

As soon as Bugsy and the mob saw that, they knew they had to regroup and put a few things on hold. As far as their situation with

Scarlet, they all knew she had to come first, and if they got any kind of static from their newest enemy Satan's Grave-Robbing Pirates, they would have no other choice but to murder them then and there, because interfering with their business, to them, was like telling a lonely sailor out on a ship, far away from his home and family, that he could no longer jack off on his own personal time. It would be a must-kill situation, and they didn't want to go through with that, because they had bigger fish to fry—namely, Scarlet. So now, the only thing they needed to do was ignore all the shit-talking going on throughout the streets and focus on the one and only Scarlet, the only one who could have possibly killed Edgar.

As they drove off in their big black Hummer, they could still feel the tension within the others, and as they looked back at them, they saw them waving their middle fingers in the air. It was very hard for Bugsy and the mob to keep their cool, and even though they had already agreed they would not act out, they decided to retaliate anyway—just to show that they still didn't give a fuck either.

Bugsy threw the Hummer in reverse and backed up into their front door entrance for the second time, making a much bigger hole than the previous one. The look on Mr. Corpse Bandit's face was priceless. Just to make him angrier, Bugsy continued to back up and reverse, hitting the front of their family's lovely established funeral home, over and over. After the damages were all said and done, Bugsy stuck his head out the window to say a few things as sped down the road, leaving their funeral home in ruins.

"Maybe you should call the real estate investors and tell them to flip your family's ragged fucking funeral home! Maybe they will put it on their television show for any funeral home buyers who give a flying fuck!"

Before Mr. Corpse Bandit and his new street organization could say or do anything, Bugsy roared the engine on his Hummer and flew down the street like a real aircraft jet plane. Mr. Corpse Bandit was now madder than ever and could not wait to get a sweet taste of revenge from their newest enemy rivals.

As Bugsy and the mob continued speeding down the road, Bugsy said what needed to be done next before they did anything else.

"Okay, everybody! Now listen up! I'm going to use this personal number of Scarlet's that we took from George back at his mammas crack house, call it up right now, and set up a date with all of us! We'll make it a real big fivesome! We'll tell her to meet all of us tonight at some lowdown hooker corner. All hookers are all about the lowdown and go down. Yeah! My kind of bitch!"

Bugsy pulled over to the side next to a Chilly Dog liquor store, whipped out Scarlet's personal phone number, and began dialing away.

"This bitch better answer the phone, too! I just want to get her out the way so we can go back and kill the fucking Munster Family at their stupid rundown funeral home! Goddamnit, I can't wait until they are all fucking dead, because we can't keep living like this, you guys. We need to start living a better and more peaceful way! Or one night, it's going to be all over for us, and you can only guess who's going to be burying our dead asses after we're gaped off the face of the fucking planet! We have a lot on our ass now! So we need to have each other's backs!"

After about five rings, Bugsy began to wonder if grandson George had deliberately given him the wrong number so he could have Scarlet all to himself. He was starting to lose his patience and wanted to punch July in the face, just because he was sitting next to him, riding shotgun. But Bugsy held it together for a little longer, and after about nine more rings, a beautiful young woman's voice finally answered. Bugsy tried his best to reel her in with his drunken, perverted, charming ways.

"Hey there, beautiful angel. This is your one and only hot 'n' sexy lover for tonight, Mr. Love Tits! Everybody knows me as the horny goat-banging monkey lover, and I would like for the two of us to get together and have ourselves a magical pussy-licking tea party! If that's all right with you, little lady?"

She could hear the others laughing in the background, not taking her business seriously, and then she wondered how such a stranger had gotten a hold of her personal phone number, and so right away, she began to ask questions.

"Okay! I don't know who the fuck this is! And I don't know how you have gotten my personal phone number! And at this moment, I really don't give a fuck! So, I'm just going to hang up now and pretend that this phone call never happened at all, and we can go our separate ways."

Bugsy knew right away that he needed to stop fooling around and start acting like a gentleman or the one and only Scarlet, whom they had been trying so hard to hunt down, would soon hang up the phone and slip out of their hands for good.

"Okay! Now, hold on, miss! Please! Don't hang up the motherfucking phone! My name is Bugsy, and those idiots that you heard laughing in the background are my associates! We got your personal phone number from a nerdy little shit named George, who just died in a burning crack house with his crack-whore mother! And I deeply apologize for our actions. We would all like to make it up to you by supporting a big part of your business. We are willing to give you five thousand dollars for just one hour of your services! We heard on the grapevine that you were the best in New York, and we are just dying to find out how great you really are, miss."

Scarlet was overjoyed that she was making a name for herself all over the rough streets of New York. She began to feel like a celebrity, and she began to talk like one too.

"Oh, please, Mr. Bugsy. You have said too much. And by the way, doll, you can call me Scarlet, and don't let that name mix you up with Betty Boop's, because I'm a bigger whore than she is, and I'll even go down longer on you, too. I do admit that I might be the queen whore of New York City, but that's because I have been in the midnight hooker show business since I was, like, twelve years old. And the fans have grown in numbers throughout the years. I guess they just can't get enough of me."

Bugsy's dick began to harden immediately upon hearing some of her references, and he couldn't wait for him and the rest of the mob to meet up with her so they could put her on ice (the dead Edgar issue).

The next thing he had to do was set up a playdate between all of them so it would be official.

"Well, I have a great idea, Miss Scarlet! I say we all get together and grab ourselves a bucket of KFC and meet at a very quiet hostel so we can all have a chance to be well introduced. Hell! I'll even bring in a high-quality video camera to *really* make you into a star! We could even be your manager and set you up with a really cool, swinging jazz band, and we'll call you guys Scarlet and the Horny Stray Cats! Oh, boy! Everyone in Whoville will go absolutely nuts over you! Oh, Scarlet! I can see it now! You are going to be the next Miss America! And I feel me and my associates can help you get to that point in your career."

Scarlet was again overwhelmed with joy and could not wait to get things started. Hearing that phone call from Bugsy was like the circuit clerk's office calling and saying that all her fines were finally paid off.

"Oh my! I don't know about the Miss America thing, but a jazz band! Now that's something I can do, because I use to be in a Jazz Band. We called ourselves the Blues Monkeys, and this guy I know by the name of Wilson London, who owned this place called the 666 Nazi Club, let us play there all the time! So, I guess the answer to your question, Mr. Bugsy, is yes! Where should we all meet?"

Bugsy already had a slight idea of where he wanted to meet, and the thought of setting up at a hostel was now totally out of the picture.

"Hey, I have a better idea than going out to some shabby-ass hostel! How about we go out and sneak into that real fine place out on Court Street. The Utica Psychiatric Center! It's been around since the 1843, and it was the first lunatic asylum in this state. My great granddaddy told me he knew a lot of friends going in and out of that place, all the time back in his day, and I just know this will be perfect for our first date! It would really bring out the thrill of old New York and what it uses to be. What do you say, my darling? Do we have a date?"

Bugsy was doing an excellent job sweeping her off her feet, and he knew if he kept playing his cards right, she would agree to a date with all of them.

"Oh my! Mr. Bugsy, you sure know how to treat a lady. I bet all the women must throw themselves at your big huge cock, because you are so charming! So, what day and time would you and your friends love to do this?"

Right then and there, Bugsy's eyes lit up like Christmas lights, and even his upside-down frown little Grinch smile came back upon his face again, lifting him, filled with joy and boner. The only thing left to do was set a time and day.

"Well, how about we meet tonight at midnight, right outside the front gate of the Utica Psychiatric Center? We will show you how to get in from there, sweetheart. And don't worry about dinner, because like I said, I'll take care of that! A bucket of KFC and a bottle of champagne with strawberries! We will all have such a blast. It will be one big Yogi Bear picnic—you will love it!"

Scarlet was happy knowing that she would be making three times as much money tonight than any other night, and because she was a businesswoman, she knew she had to capitalize on that deal as soon as she could.

"That sounds great, Bugsy! Now, you just make sure that you and your associates brush up very well for our little play date, and will have no problem."

The date was finally set, and after they all hung up their phones, it was all about playing the waiting game.

TWELVE

Midnight

It was time—time to meet Scarlet for the first time. After everything they had been through, it was all worth their while. They parked out front, waiting in their Hummer, right in front of the Utica Psychiatric Center, just as they said they would, and now all they had to do was wait quietly for her to arrive. They didn't know if she was driving or on foot, and because it was already completely dark outside, DJ RIP made sure that Bugsy stood outside so he could flag her down.

"Ay, nigga! You need to stand outside and wait for her ass! Look like a gentleman, understand? We can't afford this bitch to slip out of our fingers. We need to make sure that she always stays in our strike zone! Now, as soon as we can sneak her into this stupid fucking place—that yo stupid fucking ass sat up for all of us to go in and have a great time with this crazy-ass bitch—then the sooner we can ask questions to find out whether she killed Edger or not, and if she didn't, we can fuck her and have a great party! She will be our new best friend for every Saturday night, and if she did kill Edger, then she's a dead bitch first! And then we fuck her, and we will keep her buried in the backyard for our Saturday nights! N'am sayin'?"

Meanwhile, back at Scarlet's lovely home, she stood in front of a mirror inside a small, bug-infested bathroom, and with no lights working inside, she relied on red candles for light as she got ready for her wet-and-wild date. Already knowing she was running late made her shake nervously as she put her favorite pink lipstick on her lips, almost making her smudge pink shit all over her cheek.

"How do I look, Whiskers? Do you think I'm pretty enough to fuck?"

Her possessed Heinrich Himmler cat was still not in a good mood, and he really made her know it.

"You better not be going down there just to fuck off and do nothing! Remember, Scarlet! I need to be reborn, bitch! Without your help, I will never rise to power to kill another dirty Jew again! We must work together as a team, and so I believe you should take me with you so there will be no problem getting the bodies back to the house this time! You don't understand, Scarlet. I need the bodies so I can collect their souls and be reborn, goddamn it!"

Scarlet didn't like the idea of bringing Whiskers along, and so she had to take a moment and think about his poor feelings before she let him down easily with her stubborn-bitch rejection.

"Shut the fuck up, Whiskers! I'm not taking you with me, and that's final! You're a dead cat, and they're all going to think I'm some crazed-out bitch if I show up there with a dead cat in my arms! And besides, you couldn't help with the dead bodies, anyway! You can barely even lick your own balls, and you want me to take you with me? No fucking way, Whiskers! You just stay home and watch your fucking soap operas and try your best not to kick any cat shit out of your litter box this time, you stupid fuckhead! And maybe you should remember something too, Whiskers! Don't bite the hand that feeds you, or I swear, I'll take you straight to the pound with the rest of those fleabags! You got that, mister?"

Whiskers didn't have much of a response after hearing all that, but he still had the nerve to bitch about something anyway.

"I can't go? You got to be kiddin' me! First of all, the only reason that I kick my shit out of the box is that you haven't cleaned my shit box in three months! Open the windows in this house, bitch! I'm starting to smell my own shit rotten! Bring home some fucking air fresheners or something. I can barely breathe anymore in this shithole!"

Scarlet just ignored his needs and continued to get ready for the ball. When she was finally satisfied with her slutty image, she picked up Whiskers by his dead, shaggy fur coat and kissed him on his forehead and told him her goodbyes.

"Just shut your fucking mouth, Whiskers! Mama will be back in a bit. Goodbye!"

After using the dirty Santa Claus hat again to seal the front door shut behind her, she quickly looked to her phone and realized that she was running forty-five minutes late. Because she cared so much for her new customers, she decided to make a quick stop at her favorite friends' places before meeting up with the fellas. The most favorite place was her next-door neighbor's back porch. Her Australian dope dealer, who goes by the name of Bull-Eye Tavern, an ex-rodeo champion from Sydney, Australia, who got that nickname because he got thrown off a wild bull at bull-riding competition, and out of rage and jealousy, he took the upper half of a broken arrow that he always carried in his left boot for good luck and cut the eye out of the bull who threw him off. Scarlet was fitting to buy an eight-ball of his number-one product, called the Bastard Koala bear, and she was going to get it for everybody at the first-date party. Going empty-handed was never Scarlet's style. By doing this, she felt like she was doing her good deed for the day. Bull-Eye Tavern made her go through the back instead of using the front door was because he didn't like to draw too much attention outside the front of his house, and because he was already a drug-trafficking felon, getting caught up by the police again was the last thing he wanted.

Softly, Scarlet walked up the steps to the porch and gently knocked on the back door. She began doing her crow-cawing bird sounds, just as she had agreed to do every time she came over. Right away, Bull-Eye Tavern heard her birdcalls and the knocking at the door, and he quickly flipped on the back-porch lights to see who it was.

"Well, look who it is. That's a horse of a different color! Please, come on in!" said Bull-Eye Tavern out loud with a smile on his face as he began to unlock the door to let Scarlet in.

"Thank you so much, sir. That October weather can sure be pretty nasty. It can sometimes be hard for me to get wet and horny for somebody with weather like this."

Right away, Bull-Eye Tavern knew Scarlet didn't have cash up front for her bag of coke, and so, like usual, in return, she would give him a lousy blowjob and a reach around for his new product, the Bastard Koala.

"Oh … Scarlet! Your hands are amazin'! My God, you sure know how to earn your bag of dope. You are the true American woman, without a doubt, and if anybody disagrees, then they probably gay or from Russia! Two groups of scumbags who would never take an interest in a hot and horny lady like yourself, buts I will, and I'll even throw in a few extra dollars just to patch this deal up. But I can't keeping giving you this kind of deal like this all the time, because I'm going broke, and my rent needs to get paid too! So next time, Scarlet, you going to have to start paying cash, like everybody else, and if you don't like it, then you can take your business somewhere else, because I can only let you hustle me for so long, and I cannot let you do it anymore! You got that, miss thing?"

Just like that, Scarlet's pretty face went from a happy dick-sucking smile to a mad-and-twisted bitch look, and as she watched Bull-Eye Tavern closing his eyes so tightly and enjoying every second of his mighty great hand job, that Scarlet was so wonderfully skilled at, she quickly wiped the cum from her bottom lip and slowly reached into her purse to once again grab her favorite death weapon—the ice skate blade. Scarlet didn't really want to do it, knowing that Bull-Eye Tavern was her only dealer, and the only one she trusted as well. But still, business was business, and how he talked to Scarlet was way out the ballpark. He immediately became a new member on Scarlet's must-die list, and so, without any other thought of keeping him around for her most beloved habits, she swung away with the blade, slicing his neck wide open. The only thing Bull-Eye Tavern could hear was himself choking on his own blood, and he didn't even know why. The last thing he saw was Scarlet standing over him, with her shiny rusted blade, smirking with a smile, and he had no other choice but to listen to her last words before he slowly died, as he could no longer physically speak for himself.

"Sorry about this, baby, but there is a difference between friendship and business, and you're not acting like much of friend, being so selfish over your drugs. Therefore, it becomes strictly business, and now, my darlin' drug dealer, your time is up. Good night, bitch! And make sure you give respects to your Lord and Savior."

There was no doubt about it. Bull-Eye Tavern knew he was going to die at that very second, and there wasn't a damn thing he could do except look back at her with a smile and a middle finger in the air as she finished him off with her rusted skate blade, stabbing him directly in the eye and leaving his nerves to shake rapidly before his soul began to drift slowly away from his now-deceased body.

Time was still ticking, and Scarlet knew she had to leave the house right away. Looking to her watch, she realized it was past one. She was now over an hour late and already out the door, running down the street and hoping that Bugsy and the mob hadn't left yet, because she sure could use the money from that deal they had set up earlier over the phone.

Back at the Utica Psychiatric Center, Bugsy and the mob stood outside the front gate, waiting patiently for Scarlet to arrive. With the others keeping nice and warm in the hummer, Bugsy still stands outside like a foolish gentleman waiting to greed Scarlet when she gets there.

"Goddamn! Where the fuck is this bitch? It's been over an hour now, and it is getting cold as fuck!" yelled Bugsy as he puffed away on his cigarette while listening to the others laughing it up in the warm and cozy Hummer. He was beginning to feel angry, wondering if she would ever show. If she didn't, then they would probably have no chose but to close the case on Edgar's killer, because with all the witnesses now dead, there would be no one else to blame.

As Bugsy continued to wait, the New York weather grew much colder, and just as he was about to reach into his coat pocket to take out the card with Scarlet's personal phone number, so he could call her up and bitch her out, he heard the sound of soft footsteps slowly coming towards him. He stepped further into the streetlight, and he could see a woman standing tall with dark curly hair and a Mötley Crüe T-shirt. Just knowing Scarlet was a rocker made him cum in his underwear, and as he stepped a little bit more into the light, he could see the bright pink high heels that were making all the ruckus and the black leather pants that fit so perfectly around her beautiful waist. Now, finally seeing Scarlet for the first time ever, Bugsy could only say one thing.

"Goddamn, woman! The sexy, horny wolf within you, my love! You got my dick squirming and burning, and you make me want to get on my knees and crawl slowly to you so I can introduce my tongue to your hood-rat pussy."

Scarlet didn't know what to think about Bugsy's first approach, but still, she put a smile on her face and played it off as if she really liked it.

"Oh … Bugsy! You are so … funny … And you look so much better than you sound on the phone. I sure hope you can prove yourself worthy in bed! And where in the hell are all your friends at? They hidden or something? Call them up and tell them to get their ass out here! We have a party going on!"

Bugsy grabbed the others' attention by banging loudly on the side of the truck with his fist, to let them know that Scarlet was here.

"Hey! Guess who's fucking here, you guys."

The others were so excited to meet her that they couldn't wait any longer to jump out the truck to shake her hand. Bugsy started to get angry, as if he was just a little bit jealous. Watching the others so eager to meet Scarlet was like watching a speed-dating TV show, and it was driving him mad, to the point where he felt he had to raise his voice.

"Hey, you fucking mangy dogs! Don't be crawling all around her like a bunch of wild apes, or I'll kick the shit out of each one of you! Give this woman some breathing room, goddamnit! Show some respect! Give this bitch a chance to say a few things first before you start yapping your fucking mouths down her throat!"

The others did nothing but rolled their eyes at Bugsy as they stood still and silent, watching and waiting for Scarlet to say something.

"Oh, boys! Don't get so upset over me. I'm just like any other ordinary lady in town! Fresh of the grill and always ready to eat! Pussy, that is. I know you all like pussy, right? Maybe we can go somewhere warmer and cozier so we can get to know my pussy. Don't you think that sounds like a good plan, fellas?"

Bugsy and the mob loved that idea so much that they all blurted out their answers at the same time.

"Hell, yeah!"

"That sounds like a good idea!"

Scarlet was so thrilled that there were four of them altogether. Whiskers would be so proud of her if she managed to bring home four dead bodies all at once, she thought to herself. But to do that, she needed one hell of a scheme, because four-to-one odds might just be too much for her, and she didn't want to put her beautiful body in too much risk, because she knows that's how she made her money.

"So, fellas, is this place where you want to tie me up and make sweet, wet pussy love? I think the idea of having a fivesome orgasm inside a lunatic insane asylum is such a great idea, boys! It really makes my pussy so … fucking … wet and hot! And I'm afraid if I stay out here in the cold any longer, I'm going to lose my sweet desire of wanting to fuck some hard-ass dicks! Please, somebody, save me, and I promise I shall not let you down!"

Right away, Bugsy stepped in to speak for himself and everyone else as well.

"You know, my darling, we were supposed to ask you some very important questions before we got started, but I think we can save all that shit for later, because it's too goddamn cold out here, baby, and we need to get you somewhere nice and warm! Come on, everyone. I'm going to show you all how we going to get in this motherfucker!"

The rest of the mob wasn't too worried about how Bugsy was going to get in the Utica Psychiatric Center, because they knew he would already have his shit down, and he sure did. All it took him was a finger-to-mouth whistle at the third-floor window and a little wave with his hand, and he was in action. Luckily for everyone, Bugsy already knew somebody on the inside. Now they could relax and not have to worry about breaking in and going to jail.

"Don't worry, you guys! This crazy motherfucker I know is the night-shift janitor in this place, and he always told me I can come out to visit him anytime at night. Just as long as I bring him something to eat and something to smoke, then it's okay."

After waiting only a few minutes for his friend to come down and unlock the door to let them all in, Bugsy made sure to have a rolled-up joint hanging out of his mouth and two buckets of chicken in each hand so that when he opened the door, the guard would instantly have a smile on his face and would welcome them in nicely without acting strange about shit, like he usually did.

The fact is, Bugsy's friend, who worked as a janitor at the psychiatric center, was a little strange. His name was Reno, a drunken Marshallese from the Marshall Islands, whose breath always smelled like malt liquor every time you talked to him. There was a strange rumor that he liked to peep on random people using the bathroom, whether it was a male or female, because he said it made him feel like he was back in prison, when he was doing time for loan-shark scandals and beating up a lonely housekeeper who refused to do cleaning services for his house because she didn't want to clean anymore of his dirty jackoff bed covers, because it smelled like rotten-egg ass and Apple Jacks. Reno wasn't a married man, and he didn't have any kids. His whole life was now all about the psychiatric center. He worked there, he loved it there, and he even lived there, and he made damn sure his boss gave him the most haunted spare room in the whole facility. He said it helps them concentrate better whenever he's whacking off at night. Drunken Reno was a very strange man, but Bugsy always welcomed him with open arms in his own way.

"Hey, you full-blown drunk son of a bitch! How the fuck you been doing?"

And just like Bugsy said he would do, he did. A big old smile and a nice welcome greeting, and they were finally walking into the psychiatric center to hide from the cold October weather.

"Welcome, everyone, to my lovely work environment and my asylum home. I know you all must be thirsty, because I know I sure as hell am! I always make sure a hardworking man like myself is always stocked up on almost every hard bottle of liquor, just in case any trouble comes my way. Then I don't take it so hard."

Everybody laughed. They thought his jokes were funny, and they could smell the brandy that he took from his stocked-up liquor cabinet as he twisted the cap off the bottle and began to pass it around to the only guests that he had ever had in his home.

"Wow! Reno, you really have it going on, living in a nice place like this! I bet you bring all kinds of bitches up in here, don't you?" asked Scarlet. As the others continued to scope the place out on their own, they began to feel the same way.

"Yeah, man! Scarlet's right. I bet you do bring all kinds of bitches up in here! I know I sure as hell would be, and I would be doing it every night too!" shouted Bugsy. As soon as he took a sip of the brandy that Reno was passing all around, he could feel his body warming up from the strong liquor running through his veins, and he began to feel more relaxed and happy-home welcome, knowing that he no longer had to stand outside, waiting foolishly in the cold.

"Man alive! I should move in here with you, Reno! I can feel the evil, crazed-out energy in this place! It makes me feel good knowing that I'm not the only nut living in this fucking world. Hopefully, one day, I can retire in a nice, beautiful place just like this one."

That was just only the begging of the tour. Reno thought it would be best to show them the ballroom last, because that's where they would be hanging out for the rest of the night anyway.

"Please, come, follow me, everyone! I'll show you where we will all be kicking it throughout the night. It used to be a dance room that they called the Nutty Ballroom, and for like three hours a day, they would bring every nut in this place here to get their everyday exercise, hoping the music they played would somehow snap them back to reality and remind them about their fucked-up selves! That was the story I was told by a wise man sitting outside a liquor store. He looked like he was telling the truth, or he could have just been very drunk. I don't fucking know! And I don't fucking care too much, neither! Come on, everybody! Because the Nutty Ballroom is behind these doors, and I'm about to show you all how I get down!"

The doors that led to the Nutty Ballroom were at least ten feet tall and made from hard, hollow wood. Reno unlocked the door with all his jangling keys, then pushed the doors in slowly with all his weight to let everyone in.

The Nutty Ballroom was still in complete darkness when he opened the doors. But as soon as he switched on the lights from the inside, everything in the room became magical. The others couldn't believe their eyes. How beautiful the ballroom looked as the big, bright crystal ball above lit up the entire room. Every single inch of the place was polished and spotless, because housekeeper services were mandatory and because it was only available for insane people and not for normal assholes like the rest of the world. This warmed all of them deep inside.

Some of the things they saw in the ballroom that immediately caught their attention were the strange statues and artwork perfectly pressed up against the wall, going all around in one big circle. Two statues of rhinos, standing tall, wearing sunglasses, and holding their own dicks in their hand. A painting of an old, mad, crazy lady feeding her hundred cats and screaming at traffic. Racist Al really liked that one, because it reminded him of his own mother. Another painting of King Henry VIII and Kim Jong-un shaking hands, scrawled with blood on the bottom: "Revenge on all Americans." Everything in the ballroom was filled with unusual things. They even had upside-down statues glued to the ceiling, which kind of made everybody a little nervous, wondering if the glue was strong enough to hold all the statues, which looked so heavy.

"This place is really something, Reno! I just want you to know that, and if nobody has told you yet that you're one lucky fuck to be working here, then I'm saying it to you now! You, Reno, my friend, are one lucky fuck! You really got it made here buddy boy—I'm telling you! You can bring all kinds of fat bitches up in here!" shouted Bugsy.

There was a big amount of respect that Bugsy had for Reno, and that was because Reno came all the way from the Marshall Islands and had done so well for himself, making it in the United States. His only downfall was his drinking. Bugsy hoped, for his sake, that he didn't get out of line tonight, or he might have to kill him and take over his job and home all for himself.

Finally, after everybody had settled in and gotten comfortable in their seats, Scarlet thought it was time to really get the party started. To do so, she pulled out the eight-ball of coke, which was stained with blood from her earlier issue, poured it all on to her *Hustler* magazine, which she had rolled up nicely in her purse, and told everyone to dig in.

THIRTEEN
Bloodbath Party

Everything was going swell, and everyone was feeling great. The brandy was going down smoothly, and there was plenty of coke being passed around. The life of the party could have only been one person though—Scarlet—and throughout almost the whole night, she was talking up a storm, and everybody loved it, because her perfect-figured body was great scenery for all of them to watch, especially Reno. He couldn't stop looking at her, because she was absolutely beautiful to him, and everything that she said was like music—like he was meeting his soulmate for the first time.

"From the time I was a twelve-year-old girl, I knew I would one day be a naughty little hustler, roaming through the night and hounding every single horny asshole for his money and making their wives jealous at first sight! My dream of becoming a big dirty-bitch star has finally cum true! I may have had to kill a lot of motherfuckers just to get to the top, but that's okay, because there's nothing wrong with getting ahead in life. So if you fellas don't mind, I would like to take a moment so we can cheers to that."

It was obvious that Scarlet was getting a little tipsy, and it was only a matter of time until one of the drunken hounds made a foolish drunken move on her, and the way Reno felt about Scarlet, it was also obvious that he was going to be that lucky foolish hound—but only by playing it smart. Reno decided to wait for his big break to move in on Scarlet, and boy, he sure did, because after some more time went flying by, the Nutty Ballroom began spinning round and round for Scarlet, making her feel sick to her stomach. The alcohol had finally turned against her, and the only thing left for her to do was to get quickly to the bathroom toilet. Reno was going to be that guy to help her get there, and he knew that it was the break that he was looking for, the break that was going to get him laid tonight if he just played his cards right.

"Reno! Where's the ladies' room in this big old place?"

The sounds of an angel finally called, and off he went, running with a smile on his face, chasing after Scarlet to show her the way while the others paid no attention and continued to snort the nicely cut lines.

"Yeah! You two lovebirds have a nice time in that bathroom! We're going to drink all your fucking liquor and snort the rest of your coke! Don't forget to wear a fucking condom, or you might get the clap, and trust me, you don't want the fucking clap! You will be itching your fucking nut sack for years, and then, after shaving all the nut hairs off your balls, you will still be itching your fucking nuts! And then you will end up going mentally nuts! And when you find the bitch who gave it to you and you confront her about it, then she will think that you gave it to her, and she will go nuts on you! Goddamn! It's tough living in America!"

Bugsy was doing a very good job of being a comedian. After Scarlet had left the room, he was then the life of the party, and he was feeling on top of the world.

"Don't mind those other guys, Scarlet. They're all drunk and stupid! But you, my love, are the most beautiful thing I have ever seen."

It's just too bad that Reno picked the wrong time to holler at Scarlet, because she really let him have it. Taking his first strike at the plate wasn't what he had in mind, but he still knew he had two tries left, and if he still couldn't swing her off her feet, then he might have to spend another lonely night, with nobody else but him and his shaky drunken hand.

"Show me the fucking bathroom, Reno, right now! Or I'll slap the shit out of you so bad that you won't be able to fuck your own mother for a week!"

And so, without wasting any more time, he hurried to direct her to the nearby bathroom. He was even a gentleman enough to hold her hair while she puked chunks into the toilet. But that kind and generous man, which he was acting out so perfectly, would soon come to a crashing end. Because if there was one thing that Reno was good at, it was fucking up a good thing, and he was about to go down that path again.

"You know, my darling, I find it very attracting watching a whore puke inside a toilet bowl. It makes me want to start jerking off! It makes me want to stick my tongue down your throat so I can taste your puke breath in my fucking mouth!"

Scarlet wasn't trying to hear it. Her stomach was getting sicker and sicker every second she had to listen to Reno rambling on and on about how much he wanted to fuck her.

"Just shut the fuck up, Reno! And get the fuck out of here. I have no time to deal with customers right now! Especially you! You're just a stupid fucking slobby mob boy without a green card or education, and a sexy bitch like me will always have a horny little hound like you wrapped around my finger! Face it, Reno. You're a fucking loser! You think you're living big, but you live in a lunatic asylum, and you're a stupid fucking janitor! You will never have a woman like me, Reno! I already know what kind of guy you are, because I have been getting my pussy banged since I was a little girl, so I know what I'm talking about, and you, Reno, are going to end up back in the unemployment office, because you will no longer be able to hold your job because you're a sloppy fucking drunk, and you will have no choice but to work at a McDonald's on the weekdays, and you will be scraping dead animals off the highway on the weekends. After your hard, long, and hot day at work is finally through for the time being, you will then go home to your big old fat three-hundred-pound wife, taking care of ten screaming babies, and none of them will even be yours! Every day, you will be sitting on a piss-smelling couch because your flea-biting dog just got done taking pissing on it, and you will be rubbing your fat wife's fucking feet five times a day, watching *Murder, She Wrote* and crying and wishing that you were with someone else. That's your future, Reno, and that's where you're going to end up if you don't get the fuck out of this bathroom and give me some fucking privacy!"

That was now strike two at the plate, but Reno still had one more chance left, and he didn't want to wait until she was done puking, and so he decided to go for it all, and by saying that, I mean he went for *all the goods* and everything in between. The look of his eyes said nothing but torture and rape as he climbed on top of her and began feeling up on her tits. Scarlet wasn't scared, though. She had been in situations like this before, and she knew exactly what to do.

"You need to behave yourself, sir! You don't have to force me! Now, let's take things just a little bit slower. Don't you think that's a better idea? If you're gentle, then I'll be gentle—you got it? Now! Let's get those pants off you so we can test you out. Are you a real rocket man, or are you a five-second man? I guess we will find out right now, so please hold your head back against the bathtub here and close your eyes, because I got a surprise, and I hope you like it, because I know I'm going to."

Scarlet didn't like it at all when someone was trying to rip off the goods. According to Scarlet, pussy tastes great, but nobody can eat for free, and that was exactly what Reno was trying to do. He was trying to get a free sample to go, but Scarlet wouldn't allow it, and so, she had to do the worst thing any man should have to go through.

"Don't you worry now, baby. Mama is going to take good care of you," said Scarlet softly as she began rubbing his dick in between her fingers very slowly, hoping she could keep his eyes shut closed with her great hand work just a little longer. Then, when the moment was right, she would prepare herself to kill. But this time, she wanted to do something different. She didn't want to use her favorite ice skate blade again, as she normally did, and so instead, she decided she was going to be a little more creative. It was something that she had thought about for years, but she just never followed through with it, something she called the "kiss of death." And so, without any more of wasting time, she decided to get right to it.

Looking at his worthless four-inch cock hanging stiffly between his legs, she decided to crawl to him like a broke-down mutt without an owner, and when she got close enough that they were finally bumping heads—and when I say bumping heads, I mean from her head to the tip of his dick—and when those two heads collided, Reno already knew, because he could feel Scarlet breathing on it, and he was enjoying every second of that. Softly she begins touching her tongue to the tip of his helmet, and with just a little more pressure, she put the cock fully in her mouth and began swishing it around and around. She knew she was doing a damn good job, because she could hear the reactions from Reno as he moaned like a queer, over and over, and when she was ready, she bit down as hard as she could, breaking off his dick completely with one simple vicious bite. By the sounds of his screams, everybody in New York heard it.

The scream was so loud that car alarms were going off all over the street's, and every stray dog in town began to howl at the moon. But they were not the only ones because Bugsy and the mob were doing it. Being so drunk and not knowing what was really going on behind the bathroom doors, they just assumed that Reno was finally getting lucky and hoping that he was enjoying every second of it because when he's through, their going to want the sloppy seconds, so they can show Reno the true meaning of grateful sharing and how wonderful it is to be an American.

"I don't know what the fuck those two are doing in there, but that's the only bathroom that I know of in this place, and I'm not in the mood to go searching for the other one! Excuse me, fellas, but I think I better go over there and find out what the hell is going on, because I need to take a mad-ass piss! And if they don't let me in, then I'm going to break down the door and piss in Reno's fucking mouth! As a matter of fact, from what I remember, we were the ones who called this bitch out to come have a good time, and now Reno's trying to run off with her! Man, fuck that! Reno didn't put anything in on this motherfucker, and this bitch hasn't shown us a good time since the minute we got here! So I say we all go kick down the door and gang rape this bitch so we can show Reno how we do shit here in America. And if he starts to cry about it, then we just kick the shit out of him for acting like a fucking geek! So, are you all down or what?" asked Bugsy loudly.

As they watched Bugsy storm over to the bathroom door, they all jumped out of their seats and followed behind. All the commotion going on inside was getting louder as they got closer to the door, and Bugsy, without knocking like a normal person, decided to kick the door with his steel-toed boots instead.

"All right, you two. Times up! You all have been in there for long enough, so open up the door and come out, because I need to take a piss, and we need some good goddamn loving, too! Don't make me kick the door down, Reno, and beat your ass in front of this bitch! Because I will, and you won't like it one bit!"

Right away, Scarlet was fully alert that Bugsy and the mob wanted to kick down the door then and there, but clever as she thought she was, she continued trying to play it off that everything was cool.

"Uh …! Don't worry, you guys. He's just feeling a little bit under the weather, but we're getting him all fixed up in here, so you all don't have to worry about nothing, okay! He will be out soon, and so will I—to jump on all your guys' dicks—so stay tuned and don't go anywhere. I am definitely worth waiting for."

Bugsy and the mob didn't care. They all felt they had waited long enough for some trampy piece of ass, and they wanted Scarlet to be informed that they were not satisfied with her services, which she was supposed to deliver. So now, with all those emotions running through all their crazed-out minds, they had no choice but to kick down the bathroom door and absorb what was really going on inside.

"No! Fuck that, bitch! We are coming in now! So move the fuck out the way!" shouted Bugsy with rage. He picked up his foot off the ground and kicked in the door as hard as he could. When the door caved in, Scarlet just stood quietly at first, with Reno's body lying dead next to her, covered in blood, his dick in her hand, and before Bugsy and the mob could even open up their mouths to say anything, Scarlet immediately tried her best, in her own words, to give her explanation for Reno's dead body lying on the bathroom floor.

"Okay, fellas! This is not exactly what it looks like, but I can fairly say on my behalf that this fucking guy made me do it! I was trying to tell him in the best manner that any lady could tell a man that she's just not into him and that I was saving myself for all of you guys, but he didn't listen! He was hounding me for pussy all fucking night, and so I had to put him in his place! So please, gentlemen, is there any way you all can forgive me?"

When Bugsy and the mob saw Scarlet standing in the middle of the bathroom holding Reno's dick in her hand and his body lying next her feet, they couldn't have found anything more attractive, and so, with great honors, they took her by her hand and walked her gently out the bathroom. Scarlet's little scandal seemed to be working, but it was only a matter of seconds until she fucked it all up.

"I normally don't kill people's friends off the first time I meet them, but this guy was just getting so fucking annoying! He reminded me of this asshole I butchered the other the night at this rundown hotel. Fucking dirty old man—I think Edgar was his name—and he would never tip neither, that fucking piece of shit!"

Bugsy and the mob couldn't believe their ears. The killer of their beloved mob leader was standing right before them, and Bugsy had to respond immediately.

"So, you're the one and only, huh?" asked Bugsy all strangely.

"The one and only what? What the fuck are you talking about, Bugsy?" replied Scarlet.

"It was you, bitch, who killed our fucking boss, Edgar, and now the feelings we had for you is all changed! So, in other words, bitch, we going to kill your ass!"

As soon as Scarlet heard those words, she knew that she had to make her move quick, and she sure did. The others didn't even see it coming, when they should have. Without warning, she shoved Reno's dick, which she was holding tightly in her hand, into Bugsy's mouth. Laughter came out quickly from the rest of the mob as they stood there pointing and laughing at Bugsy, who was puking his lungs out, paying no attention to Scarlet. She easily made her escape from Bugsy and the mob and out the front door of the psychiatric center. Now, standing there looking foolish, Bugsy directed the rest of the mob to go after Scarlet.

"What the fuck are you all laughing at? Go out and kill that bitch!"

FOURTEEN

Guilty-Ass Bitch

Now that the word was finally out that Scarlet was absolutely responsible for the death of their boss, Edgar, Bugsy and the mob had no problem chasing her down until they found her and killed her. After she had made her escape from the lunatic asylum, she began running down the street as fast as she could, making sure that there was no big black Hummer trying to run her down. She did, though, hear the Hummer start up, which made her a little frightened, to the point where she had no choice but to hide behind a small bush outside a smoke shop so she could hide from Bugsy and the mob as they slowly drove by her.

But luck was not on her side. At that very moment, as the Hummer slowly creeped on by her, hiding in the bushes, the vehicle came to a halt, and everyone got out the truck with flashlights, shining them everywhere, looking for Scarlet. Her heart began racing rapidly, as she hoped Bugsy and the mob don't find her and kill her. She even tried holding her breath, thinking that is was a better way of keeping still and silent, but because she was a smoker, this didn't do anything but make her cough out loud, giving herself up and making the others immediately spot her and take her hostage.

"Hey, sweetheart, where do you think you're going? Looks like we got you now, so you better just hold still and let us viciously tear you apart! It will be a lot less painful if you just sit back and let us slowly eat your body alive!" shouted Bugsy.

Just when Scarlet thought her luck was really running out, a miracle finally came out of nowhere to rescue her. Her superhero was none other than Mr. Corpse Bandit and the Grave-Robbing Pirates, riding in their squeaky black Hearse, which was waking up the whole damn neighborhood. As Bugsy and the mob turned their attention away from Scarlet to once again confront Mr. Corpse Bandit and his reckless crew, Scarlet made her escape, but this time, she decided it would be best to tag along with a new group of psychos.

"What the fuck are you clowns doing here? Can't you little bitches see that we're in the middle of something! Now get back in that pile of fucking shit that you're driving in and get the fuck out of dodge! And you, Scarlet! You dirty fucking whore! Get your ass back here, girl, because we're not done with you yet, bitch! You did a big fucking number on us when you killed our boss, Edgar, and you should have known that you weren't going to get away with it! We were going to live large, with big mansions and fancy cars with a casino in our hands! But now, that's all over, because you fucked all that up for us! So you better get your skank ass over here so you can try your best to make it all up before we kill off your motherfucking ass, cunt!"

Mr. Corpse Bandit wasn't liking the way Bugsy was talking to Scarlet, and so he felt he needed to step in and play the superhero punk asshole and put Bugsy in his place.

"Hey, fuckhead! You're not being really nice to the lady, and our family funeral home still needs fixing! So, until you fix that, we keep the lady, and your dicks stay dry for the night, bitches! Now, you all have a nice night, and don't try reaching for your guns back in that Hummer you got back there, because we all have guns of our own, and they're locked and loaded and pointed at you right now! So, you all better not move until we're in our car and a hundred miles down the road. You got that, bitches?"

Bugsy and the mob were now steaming mad. Watching Scarlet,

the one that they had been hunting down all day, slipping out of their hands and into those of Mr. Corpse Bandit and his Grave-Robbing Pirates. To make things worse, they had to listen to Scarlet talking shit as she slowly stepped into the Hearse to get better acquainted with her new friends.

"Thank you so much, guys, for saving me from these crazy fucking animals! I wouldn't know what to do without you guys. Don't worry, though, fellas. I guess it will be your dicks that I'll be sucking on tonight and not those worthless fucking scumbags! So you all can just take me home now, because I'm super hot and horny, and I can only stay wet and juicy for so long!"

There was now a much bigger reason to kill Scarlet. Embarrassing Bugsy and the mob like that in front of new enemy rivals was very rude and uncalled for, and if it wasn't for their new rival enemies, she would already be dead. The only thing that Bugsy and the mob were left to do was just stand there and look stupid as Mr. Corpse Bandit and the Grave-Robbing Pirates drove off slowly with the woman they had planned on fucking, killing, and eating before the night was through. There was also another reason to kill Mr. Corpse Bandit and his crew: there was no way in hell that they were going to pay the estimated cost for the damages that they had caused to their family funeral home.

"All right, gentlemen! These motherfuckers want a fucking war! Then they going to get one! We will bury those fucks in their own fucking family cemetery and burn it all down when we're done, and once we get a hold of that bitch, Scarlet, it will be a whole new world for her. We just might keep her around so we can tie her up in the basement somewhere, like a hostage, and just fuck her anytime we feel like it! She will be our sex-slave whore, that does nothing but crawl around like a dog and sniffs people's asses. We will feed her raw sardines and warm water daily on a blistering hot day and rotten ice cream and cold salt water during the cold and blizzarding days."

The rest of the mob couldn't have been more excited to go after Scarlet and their new rivals, especially July. As ex-lieutenant of the US Army, he had an unmanaged plan all brainstormed in his Section 8 mental head, and he was ready to invade.

"Okay, you guys, we know exactly where they're headed, and that's straight back to their shithole funeral home, and that's exactly where we going to go so we can finish it all off! They might be expecting us, but that's okay. We will storm through them just like the greatest American soldiers did on the coastline of Normandy."

That was all the motivation they needed, and in the blink of an eye, they were all piled into the Hummer and ready to seek vengeance on Scarlet and the Grave-Robbing Pirates, speeding down the road with July behind the wheel this time, as everyone else was loading up their guns and pockets with clips and all the spear bullets they could find. It was a little hard for July to see the road at night because of all the construction that needed to be done. Potholes and faded traffic lines in the middle of almost every street made it difficult for them all to see.

"Goddamn, I can hardly see a fucking thing out here! Maybe we should wait until morning so we can see much better! We might accidentally kill the wrong people tonight—not that I would have any problem with that, because we kill innocent fuckers all the time, but if we don't start fighting back with a great competitive attitude, then we going to lose this fucking war between these assholes! So we need to fight with everything we got now, because we're not going to let some *Addams Family* faggots and a stupid whore get the best of us!"

As soon as July had said all that, the biggest, most unexpected accident occurred out of nowhere, having a huge impact on the Cannibal Mafia. As July continued to speed down the road to cross a four-way intersection, without stopping, July and the rest of the mob were T-boned by a monster-sized red pickup truck holding a trailer full of chickens, forcing their beautiful, big black Hummer, to flip in the air and crash back down hard in the middle of the mangled road. You could hear the engine echoing into the dark blue sky before it hit the ground, and everybody in the area once again just stood there, taking pictures and laughing up a storm instead of calling for medical help. Nobody in the Hummer was wearing a seat belt, and there were only three of them moving in the truck. July, the driver, was not one of them.

"Holly fucking shit, man! What the fuck just happened!" Bugsy yelled, still shaking from the horrible hit to the side. Lucky for him, though, he was sitting shotgun and wasn't driving, as usual. Unfortunately, July was, and as the others began to call out for each other to see who was still alive, DJ RIP, Racist Al, and Bugsy all saw July pinned up against the steering wheel. They began to crawl out to him to help pull his body out from the driver's seat. The airbag was popped out, and there was blood all over it. His neck was snapped, and there weren't any signs of him breathing. The rest of the mob already knew that he was dead, which brought it down to only three of them left.

Now that their Hummer was destroyed and their dearest friend, July, was dead, the only thing left to do was approach the one who was driving the truck full of chickens and put a bullet in his head, but when they all looked to see who it was, it was no surprise to them at all. The adult theater security man and fat lady, Branda Chapstick, were back again to seek their revenge for not following through on the deal that they had all discussed earlier at the theater. There was no airbag in their vehicle, and the outraged security man was slow getting out the truck as well, and as for the fat lady, Branda Chapstick, she did nothing but scream, bitching at her new security friend to kill everybody in sight.

"Don't just stand there looking all oozy, you stupid fucking idiot! Stomp their fucking ass out!"

The outraged security man was really hoping that the crash he had deliberately caused would have killed them all, but it didn't, and because he had only gotten one and still left three alive, it was now a more difficult situation for him to get out. So now he stood all by his lonesome himself, while the fat lady, Branda, continued screaming in the background for him to kill them all. Bugsy and the rest of his falling mob ran over to him quickly with their loaded pistols to cover him side to side, not leaving him with any chance to run for his life, and because the worthless security man only brought his fists to a gun fight, it was very easy for the three to shoot him down.

"Fuck you, Mr. Security Man! You should have left shit the way they were!"

But the outraged security man didn't believe that. He felt he had every right to be a crazed-out, mad lunatic, and so, without giving a rat's fuck, he continued to talk shit, and he even threw a punch, which would be the last one he would ever throw.

"All you fuck heads know you done me wrong! All I asked was for you guys to take my wife with you and kill her off, and you never kept your word, and now my wife kicked me out of the theater and told me to take this fat bitch with me so I can have more practice being a man in bed, because she says I really suck at it! So, I'm not going to waste any more of all you little bitches' time. I'm going to send you all to hell, just like I did to your friend!"

After hearing all the shit the crazed-out security man was saying out of his big yapping mouth, Bugsy and the rest of his crew knew right then and there that he didn't deserve to live any longer, and so, without looking to each other or saying a word or even thinking of anything in their minds, they turned their guns to him and opened fire. The bullets that flew out of their shiny chrome pistols pierced his skin like a hot knife going through a stick of butter, and as he fell slowly to the ground, he was still breathing softly as they stood over him, witnessing the last breaths out of his lungs, leaving him to say only a few words before he crossed over to God.

"Suck my dick, bitch …!"

All the sweet sounds of anger did nothing for him but add more bullets to his slow death, and so the last shots that were left in their pistols all went directly into his forehead.

"Say goodnight, Mr. Security Man! I never liked you and your wife's porn theater anyway! You guys always show the weakest pussy on the big screen. Pussy is supposed to be brave and reborn, not afraid to take a punishing hit from a hard stiff cock like mine! Now you go to hell, Mr. Security Man, and you make sure to tell my wife that I said it was a real pleasure killing her, and I can't wait until we both shall meet again!" Bugsy yelled.

They made sure to use every single bullet in their pistols before moving on to their next victim, and their next victim was, of course, fat lady Branda, who was still doing nothing but bitching and moaning loudly, especially at Racist Al.

"Fuck you, Al! You are a fucking cocksucker. You said we were going to be together forever and that you would never leave me and that we were going to have a picnic in the park and play bingo with my dying grandmother, but you lied!"

Racist Al felt that she deserved an explanation for everything that had happened before he strangled her with his own two fists in front of everyone.

"I was just horny, bitch! And I wanted some pussy, that's all! Nothing more!"

Quickly his hands reached out to grab her neck, and as he began to tightly squeeze, you could see and hear her spitting on her own face as she tried waving for air, but the grip of his paws was just too tight, and so she had no chose but to settle for a wrongful death.

"Okay, boss, everything is said and done here. Now, let's go finish it off!" said Racist Al, and with one vehicle still on its feet and running, they all jumped in the back of the red pickup truck full of chickens, knocking fat lady Branda out of the passenger seat and into the middle of the road. So, now with one man down, they left their dearest friend July behind lying dead in the street as they all drove off to their final destination: The Dead Cheap Family Funeral Home.

FIFTEEN

Complete Annihilation

The short drive to the funeral home was mind-wrecking for all three of them, knowing that they would be pushing forward without July. They all glanced at each other, wondering if any one of them could be next. The matchup between them and the Grave-Robbing Pirates was now on, even though they were short one person, which now made it a four-on-three death fight, because Bugsy and the rest of his mob were so heated up that it didn't matter to them. It could have been a hundred to one for all they cared; they would still fight them head-on.

"Don't worry you, guys. We are going to get all these fucking bastards! And when we're done with them, we will burn down their stupid funeral home with them still inside, and then we can finally get our hands on Scarlet so we can beat the shit out of her. Fucking that skank pussy is no longer one of my main priorities. I can't wait until all these fucks are dead so we can go back to being normal people again!" Bugsy yelled, trying his best to inspire his crew to rally.

Bugsy saw they were only seconds away from coming up on the street where the funeral home was located. He decided it would be best to pull over and park about three blocks down so they wouldn't be aware that they had arrived, and as they slowly jumped out of the red pickup truck, they realized that they had used their last bullets on their last two victims and the Uzi submachine guns that they only used once had been left back in their demolished Hummer, which was now lying on its back. They all knew then that they would have to fight them barehanded, not knowing what they might be used against them. So now they quickly searched the truck up and down, looking for whatever kind of weapon they could find to improve their chances of survival against their newest enemies, the Grave-Robbing Pirates.

After only a few minutes of digging around in a pick-up truck that didn't belong to them, hoping that the outraged security man had some kind of hard or sharp object they could use, anything good enough for a weapon, to either club someone or stab someone. Finally, all three of them had found what they needed, and they were now ready to go in and rage the night away against the crazed bitch who killed their boss, Edger, as well as the Grave-Robbing Pirates, whom they plain didn't like. So now, with nothing left to do, they headed toward their final mission, with Bugsy leading the way, holding a long Phillips head screwdriver in one hand and a sharp piece of broken glass tightly in the other. The others made sure that they were also prepared. DJ RIP had found a black steel lug wrench and bottle of gorilla glue, and with Racist Al next to him holding a ripped-out seat belt and a dead chicken to beat someone down with, it was then time to kill somebody. Now, as they all stand outside the rundown funeral home, the sudden roar of thunder sounded off with the shine of lighting following right behind it. Bugsy thought it would be best if he split himself off from the other two so that one could take the back and one could take the front.

"You two go around back and see if you can find Mr. Corpse Bandit's other two dumbass friends, and I'll take the front. Most likely, Mr. Corpse Bandit is going to try to take Scarlet all for himself, and I'm going to make sure he doesn't even get a chance to find the magic hole."

Meanwhile, inside the funeral home, Mr. Corpse Bandit was

doing exactly what Bugsy said he would be doing: trying to put the moves on Scarlet behind the closed doors of his office, and because he was a selfish asshole, who needed more privacy for him and Scarlet, he made sure Drunken Randy and Ernest unloaded all the bodies from the hearse that they had stolen a morgue last week so they could strip all the valuable goods from their bodies downstairs in the embalming room.

"That Mr. Corpse Bandit is a piece of shit! He needs to come down and help us too instead of trying to get his freak on with that bitch that we just picked up off the street! We don't even know this woman, and Bugsy might come looking for her because she belonged to him! They may have been ex-lovers or something—I don't know—but we need to start watching each other's backs around here, okay?" said Ernest, all worried and fearful. Drunken Randy made sure to slap him out of his frustration quickly so he would stop acting less like a pussy and start acting more like a man.

"Look here, you little motherfucker, I'm not going to be down here in this goddamn basement unloading and robbing these dead bodies with you if you're going to continue to act like a fucking bitch about everything! I'll leave your ass down here doing all the work yourself while I go upstairs and ask Mr. Corpse Bandit if he will let me get on a threesome with him and that crazed-out looking bitch! Haha, I would really like to see the sight of his face when I ask him that crazy shit! I'll even make sure to walk in with my parents down too! Now quit your bitching, boy, and have a drink with me. Ha, ha, ha."

Ernest found drunken Randy's lecture very humorous, and his thoughts of Bugsy trying to kill all of them was now out of his head as soon as he took a swig of Drunken Randy's cheap vodka. The two of them loved robbing corpses. It allowed them to pay off irritating bills and other personal expenses. It was only a matter of time, though, karma caught up one of them, and it sure did. Because of Drunken Randy's little lecture, Ernest was now off his guard, which made it easy for DJ RIP and Racist Al to sneak up on them from behind.

"Yeah, you're right, Drunken Randy! I am fucking worrying too much. I really need to learn how to just chill the fuck out and be more like you—drunk and careless!"

Drunken Randy was very pleased that he had talked some sense into Ernest and corrected his stinking thinking. Now he no longer had to listen to a little whining bitch all day.

"That's my boy. Now, don't you worry about a goddamn thing. We're going to be all right, and if your little friend Bugsy comes back to scare you, then we will give him an early funeral—ha, ha, ha!"

The two of them may have spoken too soon, because without any of them knowing about it, DJ RIP and Racist Al were already right behind them and ready to kill.

"What's up, little niggas! How are you all doing tonight?" DJ RIP shouted. The two were both taken by surprise so suddenly Ernest and Drunken Randy dropped their cheap-piss vodka, which they had been sharing so peacefully all by themselves, all over the ground. Just hearing the sound of the liquor bottle breaking on the hard tile floor made Drunken Randy shit a brick before anybody else could say another word.

"Hey, you two stupid motherfuckers! How dare you break into our family home and make me drop the only thing that keeps me going in life! I have to stay drunk 24/7 so I can deal with pricks like the both of you! I swear to my Lord and Savior, Jesus Christ, that if it wasn't for motherfuckers like you guys, I would be soberer than a judge on a Wet-Pussy Night!"

The entire basement smelled like foul-ass liquor from the breath of everyone who had been drinking it throughout the night. There was no fear from any of the four men, because every drop of liquor demolished it all.

"Let me tell you something about us you, two creepy ass undertaker-looking motherfuckers! We bust our asses trying to make a hustle every day, nigga, so we can live free, in peace and harmony, and always be knee-deep in madness, chaos, and violence! But there must always be some stupid motherfuckers in our way, and that's where you two fucks come in. I'm tired of dealing with it, so I'm going to end it all right goddamn now so I won't ever have to deal with clowns like you guys ever again! Killing you two off would make everything right, and it would be a great example to the community. We wouldn't have a single problem with any person in this goddamn town anymore!"

DJ RIP couldn't have been more serious while speaking to Ernest and Drunken Randy, but the carelessness and the rudeness of the Grave-Robbing Pirates would soon drive DJ RIP and Racist Al so crazy that they would have no choice but to kill them off horribly wrong. It didn't take long for DJ RIP to step in and draw first blood; with his long steel lug wrench, he reached out and whacked Drunken Randy on the right side of his cheek, making three teeth from the side pop right out, and if that wasn't good enough, he followed that hard right with a squirt of gorilla glue on top of his long, ragged hair.

"Ah! You crazy-ass motherfucker! What the fuck did you put in my hair?" Drunken Randy cried out. When Ernest saw what happened, he unleashed a side of him that he never knew he had.

"Die, you stupid motherfucker!" Ernest screamed as he ripped off one of the corpses' arms that he was unloading from the truck. The second he ripped it off, he swung it right across DJ RIP's face, breaking his nose and splattering blood all over his own suit. The second DJ RIP saw his own blood dripping from his face, it was on. All four men were now at war, and everyone in that basement at that moment went crazy on each other, giving everything they got. The fight was brutal. Chicken feathers were flying everywhere from the dead chicken that Racist Al was using to be down Ernest. Everyone was going completely nuts on each other, as if they were a bunch of drunken cowboys in a Western saloon. It was questionable who would make it out alive from their little royal rumble. However, as DJ RIP and Racist Al continued to work together, fighting side by side, they could tell that Drunken Randy and Ernest were slowly shutting down, no longer able to push on fighting because their bodies were so beaten and worn out. So, when the moment was right, DJ RIP took his final swings with his steel lug wrench right across Ernest's face—payback for breaking his nose earlier—and Racist Al ended up taking the dead chicken that he had been beating everyone down with and slapped it across Drunken Randy's face, making him dizzy and unable to stand up. When they had them both ringed up like little school kids, they quickly walked them over to the fiery cremation chamber to stick them in. They threw the men in at the same time so they could feel each other's pain as they died slowly together. Hearing their screams as they were trying to force themselves back out made them feel so glad it wasn't them, but it brought more thoughts to DJ RIP's mind.

"Man, I can't believe you let that motherfucker break my fucking nose! I thought we were going to have each other's backs?" DJ RIP cried out, but Racist Al couldn't care less, and so he just rolled his eyes and tried his best, in his own words, to make him feel better about the situation.

"Keep your fucking mouth shut, boy! You know what you signed up for, so don't start crying and bitching about how you were done wrong! Goddamn, you sound like a wounded veteran who just returned from war, always blaming somebody for your own reckless decisions that you made in life! You better screw your head on tighter or I'm going knock it right off your shoulders, and when I'm done with that, I'll send you to go work in the fields, picking strawberry with all the Mexicans! They could always use a cotton-picking negro like you!"

That was the straw that broke the camel's back. DJ RIP had heard his last racist remark that he was ever going to hear from Racist Al ever again.

"All right, you little bitch ass nigga! I done told you about how I feel about your racist mouth, and now I'm going to have to put an end to your wise cracker ass!"

DJ RIP whacked him upside his head with his new lucky steel lug wrench and followed it up with a hard kick to his chest, knocking him into the embalming table and on to the hard tile ground. Racist Al was pretty shaken up after that, and as he got back on his feet, he took the dead chicken that he was holding so tightly in his hand and began coming after DJ RIP with it, swinging away and beating his head. It was a very close and brutal fight, but unfortunately, steel is much harder than a dead chicken, and so, as the two continued to beat each other's brains out, Racist Al's legs finally caved in, and as he slowly hit the ground from all the hard hits that he was brutally taking from the steel lug wrench, he could only say a few words as he looked up at DJ RIP standing over him, waiting to finish him off with the last hits of his new favorite toy, which he now called "Blacky the Steel Wrench Cracker Killer."

"Take this dead chicken home with you, boy. I know how you black folks love your chicken. Haha …"

And so, without saying a word, DJ RIP bashed his head a few more times to end it all for good. The war between the north and south was now over, and as DJ RIP looked around the basement floor, he could fairly say that the war between them and the Grave-Robbing Pirates was almost over as well, but there was no telling yet how everything else was going upstairs, where Bugsy was supposed to be handling his part of the business.

During the whole time that DJ RIP was fighting off the Grave-Robbing Pirates and ending a personal friendship with Racist Al, Bugsy was breaking into the side window of the funeral home, which led to the main living room upstairs. After looking around to make sure everything was clear, he easily made his way through. There was nothing going on in the living room—everything was quiet—but as he got closer to the hallway that led him to the other three rooms of the funeral home, he quickly put his ear up to each one of the doors to see if he could overhear Scarlet and Mr. Corpse Bandit having the time of their lives.

"I really hope that you like it here at my family's funeral home. Everything here is so peaceful and quiet. Maybe it's because God is among us, or maybe it's just because everybody is fucking dead! But what I do know is that you're a very lovely lady, Scarlet, and I would really like to be all up inside you."

Another horny motherfucker trying to get up her skirt, but she didn't allow that to bother her. She barely knew the guy, and because of that, she didn't know exactly what his true intentions with her were, other than he wanted to fuck her. But Scarlet didn't care about that part, because there was usually a freebie for every new customer anyway. A "client's free sample" is what she would call it, but you had better have cash if you come back for seconds. This case was a little different. Scarlet could sense the control-freak evilness through Mr. Corpses Bandit's bad vibes, and so, she tried to delay all sexual activity by frequently asking questions, one after another.

"I'm so sorry, but what was your name again? I have fucked so many men in my life that it's hard for me to remember who everyone is. Where did your other friends go? Maybe you should go look for them while I stay back here and freshen up. If you want to fuck me the right way, sir, then you need to give me a few moments to get my pussy cat nice and juicy for you. Is that okay, baby?"

Mr. Corpse Bandit had no problem allowing Scarlet to proceed with her request, and as he shut the door behind him to leave Scarlet in privacy, he was suddenly face to face with the one and only Bugsy. There were no words that needed to be spoken, and so the two men, without even saying a word, began throwing punches left and right.

They were going at it nonstop, and nobody was coming in between them to stop it. The only protection that Mr. Corpse Bandit had was his own bare fist, while Bugsy used the Phillips screwdriver and the sharp broken glass as his own personally made brass knuckles. But he wasn't cutting him as deeply as he wanted to. The two tools that he had chosen for the rumble were going to completely fail, which gave Mr. Corpse Bandit the advantage to regain control of the fight. Mr. Corpse Bandit didn't want to get beat in his own family funeral home. That would be total embarrassment to his high eagle of the corpse robbing pride that he was.

Bugsy knew that his reputation was also on the line, and he couldn't allow the Cannibal Mafia name to be printed on the front page of the newspaper, saying that they had been defeated by the newest rivalries, the Grave-Robbing Pirates. So now, with all those thoughts pouring into both of their crazed-out minds, they now fought even harder to stay alive to see who would remain the leader of their pack.

During the struggle of their fight, DJ RIP made his way up the stairs from the basement. He heard all the commotion going on in the living room, and as he was scoping out the fight between Bugsy and Mr. Corpse Bandit, he figured Bugsy had it all under control, and so he left the two to duke it out all by their lonesome while he looked for Scarlet in the other rooms. DJ RIP's lucky guessing was always on target, and the first room he looked in was the right one. The second he walked in, he caught Scarlet trying to make an escape through the window. But luckily again for him, he was there to stop her.

"Hey, ho! Where in the fuck do you think you're going? Are you just going to leave like that without even telling a nigga goodbye? Where's your fucking manners at, bitch? Since we're all alone now, maybe you can give a nigga some love? I have been through hell looking for your trailer-trash ass, and now you better give me some pussy! It would only be fair!"

Scarlet couldn't believe that she had been stopped right before making her escape through the office window. Now she had to give her full attention to DJ RIP, who was standing directly behind her.

"Oh, my! DJ RIP, don't do nothing foolish now! Maybe we can work something out? I have the time, and I know you do too."

There was no way that DJ RIP could turn down pussy. Any black man who turns down pussy in his neighborhood growing up was always considered mentally retarded, a Jew out of Israel, or just another fag on the street driving for attention, wanting to be cool, and there was no way DJ RIP was going to allow anybody in the hood to think differently of him.

"Hell yeah, bitch! You know I got the time, but I don't have the money, and I probably would have if you didn't kill our fucking boss! So, if you want to make it out of here alive, bitch, then you better give up the goods! Don't make me come down there now and make me wring your chicken head up and force you to give me the goods, because I might accidentally kill you! But I guess your pussy taste just as good if it was dead! I wouldn't want to feel you breathing on me anyway!"

As clever as Scarlet was, she knew exactly what to do in a situation like this, and so she continued to do what she had always been so good at doing, and that was knowing how to put a man at ease.

"Trust me, Mr. DJ RIP, my pussy is much better wet than it is dry. Now, if you just give me a chance to prove myself to you, I'm sure I could make the rest of your night worth your while, and if you kill off that slave-driving asshole Bugsy, then we could truly be together forever. I have seen the way he treats you around others! He barks orders at you like some slave on a farm! Tell me now, baby, are you a man in charge, or are you just another black slave under another white man's thumb? You going to have to make a choice! Pussy or bro? What's it going to be, DJ RIP? What is your answer going to be?"

The choice between the two wasn't easy for DJ RIP, and he did feel that Scarlet was right on some parts, although she could have been just twisting up his mind with lies. But still, DJ RIP was a man of risk, guts, and glory, and there was no way that Neither Bugsy or Scarlet was going to punk him out in any kind of way.

"Okay then, bitch! Let's both make our escape through the window now and leave these two fucks here to kill each other off! We can run away to Paris together, my love, and never return to New York City ever again!"

Scarlet loved his offer. It was a lot better than being dead. But deep inside, she knew that she had no desire to fall in love with anybody at any time soon, and so, she continued to lead him on with her own skeptic ways so she could set herself up for the perfect opportunity to kill him off.

"Oh my, Mr. DJ RIP. I always wanted to go to Paris! We should go right now before one of the others comes up here! We don't want nothing to do with those assholes anymore, do we, baby? You would rather have a nice wet pussy instead, huh, honey? Yes, you would. Now, let's get the fuck out of here! So, please lead the way before they burst in the door and capture me, and then we will never be able to fuck!"

After hearing those words out of Scarlet's mouth, he dashed toward the window to lead the way out into the crisp night. Although only one thing went wrong. One of the number-one rules on the streets, which DJ RIP had stupidly forgotten, was never to turn your back on a crazed-out bitch with mental problems, because as soon as his back was facing her, she knew it was perfect timing for execution, and, so once again, gripping her favorite ice skate blade, which she had used to kill so many of her victims, she raised it to the sky, held her breath, and drove it into the back of his neck and all the way out his throat. Watching him drop to the floor as his nerves did all the shaking and dangling on the ground, she wondered if she should gather his body for Whiskers so she wouldn't have to hear him bitch later tonight.

Meanwhile, out in the living room, where Bugsy and Mr. Corpse Bandit were still squaring off, there was still no telling who would come out on top, and as they continued to fight, on and on, growing more and more tired, Mr. Corpse Bandit ended up making a horrendous mistake on his own funeral home grounds. Thinking of a way to kill Bugsy off, he grabbed the fish tank off the shelf. It was lit up like Christmas lights and was filled with nothing but dead fish and old-ass fish food floating on top of the water. As he raised the fish tank over his head to chuck at Bugsy, he couldn't throw it off quickly enough, because he just had to have the last words before he kills off his enemy.

"Suck my fucking dick, Bugsy! I'm going to make sure that your tombstone reads in perfect American English, 'Here lies Bugsy, the biggest faggot mobster of all time and whose very first piece of ass was his own whore mother.' Ha, ha, ha, ha, ha!"

If only he had thought quickly enough, he would have seen Bugsy's Phillips screwdriver flying out of his hand from him darting it so quickly into his eye, making Mr. Corpse Bandit drop the fish tank onto his head, breaking his neck as he fell hard to the living room floor. Water flooded everywhere, making the floors squeak everywhere you stepped.

"Looks like I will be the one who takes over this city, motherfucker! Now, you lay there in your own blood and think about what you did and how God could ever forgive an animal like you!"

After saying his last words to his victim, he turned his head toward the room, where he had seen Mr. Corpse Bandit come out. He wondered who else awaited him behind the door. If it was Scarlet, then he would have no choice but to punish her with death for the troubled she has caused. Trying his best not to make too much noise from the wet floors as he softly made his way toward the room, he heard movement, inside like someone dragging a dead body across the floor. Bugsy knew what it sounded like. He had grown up around it his entire life. So now as he stood face to face outside the door of the room that he needed to exit, he turned the knob and pushed it right open. It was exactly who he thought it was: Scarlet. She was trying to make her escape out the side window with DJ RIP's dead body in one hand and a bloody ice skate blade in the other.

"Stop right there, bitch! You're not going anywhere!"

At that moment, there was no telling what would happen between them, but as he looked into Scarlet's eyes as she slowly turned around, he knew that he had pissed off the wrong bitch and that he would never hear the end of it until he allowed her to say whatever it was on her mind, and so, he did nothing but freeze up stiff like a little girl and listen to everything that she needed to let out of her crazed-out ass. Everybody looked to be dead anyway, so he had all the time in the world to hear out her side of the story.

"Look here, Mr. Bugsy! I have already been through some crazy shit tonight, and I don't have the time to stand here and talk to you! All that I ever wanted in life was just to be treated like a normal person so I could live peacefully, but guys like you must always take that away from me! You remind me of my drunken father growing up, and that makes me want to stab your throat until you're dead. I never had the perfect childhood that every little girl wants! Instead of playing with dolls, my parents would make me play with cat shit out of the cat box, because Daddy couldn't afford his daily dose of liquor, and my mother would just sit there in her rocking chair, rocking away and talking about every dick she ever sucked and how I needed to work myself up to be just like her in order to be a real woman! My sweet mother said every little girl should practice with her father first so she can understand her true roots and where she came from. So, every day after school, I would practice with my father, and sometimes my mother would join us in the mix during everything, but then Daddy would get mad because she was too old, and he would rather have a younger lady like myself to fulfill his needs. That didn't last long, though, because then Mommy soon got mad, which cost my father his life. Chopping my father into pieces with a big red ax on the day before Christmas was my mother's first present to me as a ten-year-old girl! My fourth-grade teacher, Mrs. Brownie Baker, could always smell the nasty nut stain cum in my hair, and she would keep me after school so we could take turns licking it off. It always turned me on, because none of the boys my age were yet interested in sex, because they were too busy playing with Crush dummy toys and reading *Goosebumps* books. I didn't like those kids anyway. They would always act like such children, and they had no respect for the fatherland of their country! So I had no choice but to quit school, and I made sure to fuck my teacher, Mrs. Brownie Baker, and my principal one last time before I went home to kill my mother! They were so thankful that I thought of them before I dropped out, and my mother never saw her death coming from behind as I took a baseball bat and batted her head as hard as I could, over and over and over again! Blood was all over the walls, ceiling, and floors, and it made me want to fucking masturbate over and over and over again! Now, I think you should let me slip through this window, Mr. Bugsy, and go your own way, because I can feel your heartbeat from over here, and I know you scared of me, boy! *You* know this crazed-out bitch can bring you death! So go home while you still have the chance."

All Bugsy could do was stand there in silence, wondering how he was going to deal with Scarlet's crazy ass. Thoughts of letting it be and just going home did indeed cross his mind, but the fact that he'd already gone through hell just to find her made him want to stand his ground and finish what he'd started. He had no choice but to continue to carry out Scarlet's death all the way to the end. It was the least he could do after dragging his mob into this mess just to get killed. He must now avenge their death if he wanted to continue without any guilty conscience.

"I'm not going anywhere, bitch! I'm going to stay right here with you so we can be close friends. I'm so sorry to hear about your dead daddy! Maybe now I can be your daddy! I'll enjoy feeling up your body just like he did! Ha, ha, ha!"

The rage within Scarlet after hearing Bugsy trash-talking her childhood life made her eyes widen. She raised her bloody ice skate blade to the sky one last time. As Bugsy looked back at her with his bloody Phillips screwdriver held tightly in his hand, he knew that he was ready, and that one of them in that room was surely going to die, but as the seconds continued to pass, it was all over—not just for one of them but for both.

Neither of them even saw it coming. They were ambushed with flying bullets coming from almost each direction, and their bodies both hit the ground instantly, leaving them both dead without even saying any last words.

Who could have done this, you properly wonder? Another new rival gang rivalry in the streets of New York City, a gang well known for murder, burglary, and company fraud, a gang that went by the name of the No Rent Movers, a non-licensed repo/moving company that rode around killing people and robbing houses, telling authorities their victims hadn't paid their rent and that they were sent by the state to clean them out.

"All right, assholes, don't grab any stupid shit. Just grab whatever valuable goods that could possibly pay your fucking rent!"

It seemed that the Grave-Robbing Pirates finally got a taste of their own karma, because now, instead of them digging through other deceased bodies, someone was now digging through theirs. It was just too bad that Scarlet and Bugsy had to be part of it, not to mention everyone else who died.

My God rest their souls.

About the Author

Dark fiction horror novelist Danny Salazar unleashes his second novel "sick and twisted" to all the wonderful horror fans throughout the world and hopes you all enjoy it dearly. Danny Salazar was born in Moline Illinois and now resides in Maui Hawaii. He wants again hopes all his readers enjoy the book and encourages everybody to not try any of the events of this novel at home. Thank you and enjoy.

Printed in the United States
By Bookmasters